Secret Son...

"A first grader was suspended from Palm Mesa Elementary School today when a teacher claims she saw him cause a flying fork to change course in midair," the reporter announced. "Let's talk to the boy's mom."

The camera cut to a tall slender woman trying to steer a boy down the front steps. Chance's breath caught in his throat.

It was his lady. Even after all this time, there was no mistaking her.

"Mrs. Blayne?" asked the reporter. Chance's heart sank. Apparently she was married. But wasn't that obvious, since she had a child? "What do you think of the claim that your son has mental powers?"

"Harry's a normal kid," she snapped. "I think everyone is making too much of this."

As she led the boy away, he glanced back, and for the first time, Chance saw his face. Small and impish, just like his mother's, except for his eyes. Chance sat bolt upright.

Impossible. Unthinkable. He looked closer. Unmistakable. As the child looked up, his eyes glimmered silver. Just like Chance's own.

ABOUT THE AUTHOR

Jacqueline Diamond has led past lives as a
journalist and a television columnist. She wishes
she had led a past life as a financial wizard.
She and her husband live in Brea, California,
with their two sons, Ari and Hunter, who have
no magical abilities, but get into plenty of
mischief anyway.

Books by Jacqueline Diamond

HARLEQUIN AMERICAN ROMANCE

218—UNLIKELY PARTNERS
239—THE CINDERELLA DARE
270—CAPERS AND RAINBOWS
279—A GHOST OF A CHANCE
351—BY LEAPS AND BOUNDS
406—OLD DREAMS, NEW DREAMS
446—THE TROUBLE WITH TERRY
491—A DANGEROUS GUY
583—THE RUNAWAY BRIDE
615—YOURS, MINE AND OURS
631—THE COWBOY AND THE HEIRESS
642—ONE HUSBAND TOO MANY
645—DEAR LONELY IN L.A....
674—MILLION-DOLLAR MOMMY

Don't miss any of our special offers. Write to us at the
following address for information on our newest releases.

Harlequin Reader Service
U.S.: 3010 Walden Ave., P.O. Box 1325, Buffalo, NY 14269
Canadian: P.O. Box 609, Fort Erie, Ont. L2A 5X3

Jacqueline Diamond

DADDY WARLOCK

Harlequin Books

TORONTO • NEW YORK • LONDON
AMSTERDAM • PARIS • SYDNEY • HAMBURG
STOCKHOLM • ATHENS • TOKYO • MILAN
MADRID • WARSAW • BUDAPEST • AUCKLAND

For Jennifer Poling, Michelle Thorne, Janet Carroll,
Anne Noyes, Julie Kim, Melissa Becker,
Michelle Harned, Mike Gibb, Leanne DuPay,
Heather Osborn and all the other wonderful bookstore
people who help readers find my stories!

ISBN 0-373-16687-7

DADDY WARLOCK

Copyright © 1997 by Jackie Hyman.

Prologue

The house looked like a castle, with its stone walls, battlements and turrets. But what was it doing in a canyon in Southern California, and what kind of man would own such a place?

"You're sure this is the right address?" Tara Blayne asked as she and her friend Denise approached in the moonlight. Nearing the rounded front door, they roused no reaction from the two guards in beefeater uniforms who stood with lances crossed, and she realized the pair were holograms. "Could you have mistaken the number in the dark?"

"I don't think so. But I'm not sure whether the street sign read Achilles or Apollo." Denise huddled into her witch's robe.

It was more than half an hour since they'd turned off Sunset Boulevard onto a series of narrow canyon roads that wound around until Tara no longer remembered which way was north or south. A narrow driveway had brought them to this castle half-hidden in a grove of eucalyptus.

Lanterns flickered from the trees. No lights shone from inside the castle, perhaps because there didn't appear to be any windows. Only the presence of a dozen cars parked along the driveway provided some reassurance of normalcy.

Denise eyed their surroundings uneasily. "It's a private home, obviously, but even for the Hollywood Hills it's kind of strange. Maybe we should leave."

"You're kidding! After that long drive? And the trouble we went to, finding costumes?"

Tara had splurged more than she could afford on her long skirt, low-cut blouse and black bodice. If she had to work as a serving wench in real life, she might as well look like one on Halloween. "Besides, I'm starved. I spent so much on my costume, I had to skip dinner."

The money she earned waiting tables didn't stretch far, especially since it had to cover business classes. But even though Tara had resolved to accept her father's urging and pursue a serious career, she couldn't resist indulging in pure fun once in a while.

"I can't understand why I let you drag me into situations like this." Denise, a hairdresser, was invited by her clients to numerous parties but rarely accepted without prompting. "We don't even know who lives here. He might be some kind of weirdo."

"You said he was a friend of a client," Tara pointed out.

"More like a friend of a friend of a client," grumbled her pal. "And what does that prove? Even criminals' friends get their hair cut. And permed and colored, in this case."

Tara decided to try a new tack. "Look at all the trouble he's gone to." She patted one of the walls, which on close inspection was made of foam. "He's transformed the whole front of his house. The guy must be rich, which means the food probably is, too."

Denise straightened her peaked hat. "Okay, I'll go as

far as the refreshment table. But if the people act peculiar, we're leaving.''

''If they're that strange, I'll get out and push the car to make it go faster.''

In spite of herself, Tara felt a tremor of uncertainty as they stepped through the open door. Inside, the room was dark. From the echo of their footsteps, she gathered that it must be large, but how large, she couldn't tell.

Tiny lights marked a meandering pathway across a smooth wooden floor. On either side, skeletons dangled, shrunken heads grimaced and pumpkins leered in rotating flashes. Something slimy trailed across their necks, making them both shriek.

''This guy's got a sick sense of humor,'' Denise muttered.

''Or he's a real party kind of guy.'' Tara hoped she was right, and their host was simply getting into the spirit of the holiday.

Voices drifted from beyond the room, and a moment later the two women stepped into a courtyard full of people. The atrium, open to the sky, was filled with lanterns, long tables of food and costumed partygoers.

Soft music—Tara recognized it as *Symphonie Fantastique*—soothed her anxiety, and the scents of night-blooming flowers mingled with the tantalizing aroma of spicy food. Their host was clearly both generous and sensual.

He also owned a house that might have come from her dreams. In the lantern glow, arched windows and undulating stucco walls made it resemble a palace from the Arabian Nights. As if to complete the fantasy, a curving staircase led to a small tower atop the rear wing. It seemed to have been transported from a magic realm, a place of sorcery and surprises where anything could happen.

She bit her lip to stop the unwanted musings. As her father always said, the people who succeeded were the ones who kept their noses to the grindstone. After dropping out of college and wasting several years on low-paying jobs, Tara intended to make more responsible choices from now on.

"You were right! It's a terrific party." Denise gave a little hop that set her bushy red hair bouncing. "Look at the cute guys! What do you think of that one over there?"

"That one" was a blond surfer-type. "Just your style," Tara observed.

In fact, most of the men were Denise's style—fresh-faced and cheerful. Handsome, too, in their disguises as superheroes and swashbucklers.

The women were striking enough to make Tara feel clumsy by comparison. Whether dressed as Pocahontas or harem dancers, they moved with easy self-confidence, and several were downright voluptuous.

All her life, people had told Tara she should be grateful for her tall, slender frame. Well, those people didn't have to do daily battle with elbows and knees that had a mind of their own.

Not to mention mouse-brown hair so limp that, in desperation, she'd had Denise cut it into a short mop. Even so, it could only be tortured into shape with massive infusions of mousse.

A sudden hush drew Tara's attention to the top of the staircase. On the balcony stood a commanding figure in a tuxedo, a black hat and a scarlet-lined cape.

What riveted her was not the costume but the man himself. His features were chiseled, and even the tailored restraint of the tuxedo failed to disguise the power of his shoulders and upper body.

Beneath a half mask, silver eyes raked the assembly. He stopped abruptly, focusing on someone as if startled. With a jolt, Tara realized he was staring at her.

Conquering the urge to retreat, she shot him her most mischievous smile, the one that had always cut short her father's tirades about irresponsibility. Inevitably, it would send him storming away, but at least he would leave her in peace.

This man, however, had no intention of leaving her in peace. His mouth twisted wryly and, his eyes fixed on her face, he descended the steps so smoothly, he might have floated just above the surface.

"That's a neat trick," murmured Denise. "I wonder how he does it."

"Enchantment," Tara said as the man approached.

Bending over her hand, he brushed it lightly with his lips. Heat danced across her skin and radiated deep inside her.

The man was dangerous. And irresistible.

His silver gaze caught hers, and Tara read a question there. It made her breath catch in her throat.

She didn't know why she was reacting this way. In her twenty-two years, she'd never felt as completely engaged by a man as she did by this one.

His mind seemed to reach inside hers, brushing across her inhibitions and dismissing them. With a rush of excitement, she felt him touch the private places that she shared with no one.

He was there in a field of wildflowers that had grown behind her childhood home outside Louisville, Kentucky. A spring breeze ruffled her cheeks as she lay against him, feeling the tautness in his muscles as he pulled her close.

Then they were walking arm in arm along a path in an ancient forest. Ahead of them, in a glade, lay a tiny thatched cottage. Tara had never seen this place before, and yet it was home.

She blinked, and saw that the man was giving his head a light shake as if to clear it. What had just happened between them?

"Are you our host?" Denise asked. "I hope you don't mind, but we were invited by a friend of a friend."

"I don't mind at all." The man held Tara's hand as if reluctant to let go. "The party wouldn't have been complete without you. Have you eaten yet? Or sampled the punch? It's my own recipe."

"A magic potion?" Tara asked. "To entice the unwary?"

A smile revealed a crease in his cheek, reminding her of an old-time movie star. "There is a special enchantment tonight," he said, "but it has nothing to do with the punch."

The rapid beating of her heart informed Tara that his magic *was* working. But, of course, it wasn't really magic, just natural chemistry.

"Do I have to divine your name with the help of sheep's entrails?" she asked. "Or could you just tell it to me?"

He threw back his head and uttered a deep, rumbling laugh. "I like a woman who gets to the point. But tonight I'm not my usual self. Tonight I am the Magician."

With that pronouncement, he clapped his hands in a staccato sequence. Colored sparkles shot into the air from both sides of the courtyard, a fountain in the center bubbled to life and the background music segued into the dark tones of *The Phantom of the Opera.*

"How did you do that?" asked Tara as the other guests applauded.

"Witchcraft, of course," he said. "And what is your name? Or shall I invent one that befits your costume?" His gaze traveled down her low-cut blouse, registering appreciation. To her dismay, she felt her nipples tighten and her skin flush.

"If you call me Wench, I'll slap that hat right off your head," she growled.

Amusement gleamed in his silver eyes, which, close up, had a faintly exotic tilt. "I wouldn't dream of it. I shall call you My Lady."

"I've had enough of this nonsense." She whipped her hand from his grasp. "If you don't care to exchange names, I think I'll go try some of that food."

Denise looked horrified at Tara's abruptness. "She skipped dinner," she explained apologetically.

"And I must greet my other guests." The Magician bowed. "Until later."

As he moved away, others crowded around him. Denise frowned at Tara. "Why were you so rude?"

"The man's kissing my hand and he won't even tell me his name?" She led the way toward the refreshment tables. "He sounds like exactly what I don't need."

She didn't want to admit the effect the man was having on her nervous system. His focus on her had been so complete that she'd felt as if he were invading her mind. She kept getting the odd sense that at a subliminal level they already knew each other.

The scary part was the premonition that if she yielded to him, even for a little while, her life would rocket out of control. Tara didn't want to lose control.

"I wonder what he does for a living," she mused as they filled their plates with stuffed mushrooms, crab cakes and tiny pizzas. "Maybe he performs magic tricks at clubs."

"You don't afford a house like this by giving little magic shows," said Denise. "But he doesn't look much older than we are. Maybe he's an actor or something. That would explain why he's wearing a mask."

Tara doubted the man could be famous. With those silver eyes, she would have recognized him in spite of the disguise.

A blond pirate interrupted their discussion as he introduced himself to Denise. A couple of his friends wandered over and someone asked Tara to dance.

She spun around the courtyard with one partner after another, scarcely noticing them. Denise was dancing with the blond fellow, who wore a rakish scarf knotted around his temples. The two seemed happily lost in each other, although that didn't mean much, since Denise tended to change boyfriends as often as she changed lipstick colors.

Everywhere Tara turned, her gaze alit on the Magician. He stood out from the others, not by his height or his costume but because of his intense watchfulness.

He seemed to be aware of every move she made, even when he was deep in conversation. His attention bathed her like a warm spring, smoothing away distractions, eddying and teasing, drawing her closer.

Tara's wariness eased, and she began to feel safe whenever her partners whirled her close to the Magician. He was the source of the warmth, the center of gravity, the solid ground just beyond the whirlpool.

As the world lost its hard edge of reality, the walls of the house shimmered and the air tingled like champagne. If Tara got any more light-headed, she might fly.

Wherever she gazed, the Magician was there. His

knowing smile lingered in her mind, overlying the faces of the guests.

At last she found herself dancing in his arms, without any memory of how she had come to be there. His hand imprinted itself on her waist as he led her through a waltz.

Tara had never fancied herself much of a dancer. She was too awkward, her elbows plowing into whoever ventured nearby, her feet tangling with her partner's.

But tonight she became Cyd Charisse, scarcely touching the flagstones of the terrace. The man of mist and magic merged with her and they skimmed along with instinctive grace.

In an inexplicable way, she felt more herself than she had ever been. Tara's whole life, since her mother's death when she was twelve, had been a struggle between the venturesome self nurtured in childhood and the practical Tara born of her need to please a rigid father.

But tonight, the Magician's power fused the conflicting parts of her spirit. Tonight, boldness and risk taking formed a sure path to success.

Although his movements mirrored her slightest shift as they danced, her host comported himself like a gentleman. He made no attempt to nuzzle Tara's neck, as a previous partner had done, or to brush her mouth with his, or to press his arm against the swell of her breasts.

Yet his nearness enveloped her, his body carving the space around her. Tara had never experienced such heightened awareness, all of it riveted on one man.

They moved away from the others, dancing into a shadowed alcove. In response to their nearness, the space became infused with an amber glow. She saw that he was leading her toward the curving staircase.

"Where are we going?" Tara murmured.

Concern played across the man's face. "Have I misunderstood? Don't you wish to be alone with me?"

"But we're not alone," she whispered. "Together, we form something larger than ourselves." She didn't know where the words came from but they seemed true.

The Magician regarded her with surprise. "Yes, I sensed that when I saw you."

Before she could reply, his hands cupped her face. Beneath his gaze, Tara no longer felt knobby and coltish. Her muscles lengthened; her joints smoothed; from her shoulders to her fingertips, her bunglesome self fused into womanhood.

The Magician lifted her as lightly as dandelion fluff. Again, Tara had the impression that their minds intertwined as he mounted the stairs. She was part of his muscles, reveling in the power to carry her, and she shared the elation of his spirit.

A door swung open at their approach and they entered a round room. It must, she realized, be the tower. The chamber was empty, right down to its polished wooden floor.

"Bedchamber!" The Magician spoke into the air.

Velvet curtains whispered across the windows. From the rear wall descended a broad bed, while hidden portals slid aside to reveal an oak armoire.

Tara had the impression that the sensual fabrics and sleek woods had been selected to suit her sensibilities. The room had been waiting for her.

The Magician set her down, his eyes gentle behind the mask. She wished, fleetingly, that he would take it off, but then it didn't matter. What she knew of him went far deeper than what could be seen in his face.

The strangest part was that she knew he was experiencing both the same fire of longing and the same reluctance to yield to it. She knew he was afraid of hurting her, and uncertain of what she meant to him, and that he stood at a crossroads in his life.

With a stab of insight, she saw that somehow she had been sent here to change him, and he to change her. But in what way? How could their thoughts be so intertwined at this moment, while they yet withheld so much of themselves, even their names?

The Magician's hand caressed her hip, burning through the fabric. Tara ran her finger along his jawline, and felt a shiver of response.

She touched the faint stubble of new-grown beard. As if they were connected by electric wires, she experienced not only what lay on the surface but also his rush of hunger, his disbelief, his eagerness, his doubts.

Then her eyes met his and, with a jolt, she saw that he was inside her mind, too.

He was experiencing her smoky rush of longing, the tightening in her breasts, the melting in her marrow. The double awareness was overwhelming, for both of them.

Tara's only previous experience with lovemaking had been a few fumbling encounters with a college classmate whom she'd briefly imagined she loved. She had felt nothing like this soaring eagerness to arouse and share and merge.

Her partner smoothed the blouse low over her shoulders, his thumbs caressing the exposed tops of her breasts. Tara wound her arms around his shoulders.

She drew the man against her, mouth meeting mouth in explosive hunger. The moment they connected, all hesitation vanished.

With a shrugging movement, his upper arm pushed the mask back and knocked off his hat. But with the curtains

blocking the moonlight, she could see nothing except the
outline of his face.

The Magician. It seemed like name enough, just now.

Memory and delight flowed together as they slipped
from their clothes and tangled together on the bed. There
was no order to their passion, just thigh wildly brushing
thigh, his lips against her nipple, her hands molding his
shoulders, his body responding with hot abandon.

She shared his wonder, and his torrent of need. She
knew he must have penetrated her mental recesses, as
well, finding the wall she'd flung up to protect herself
from her father's disapproval and from anyone else who
might try to control her life, the barrier that had vanished
for this one amazing night.

Only one night? she wondered. But it wasn't like that.
All the nights they had known belonged to both of them.
Past and future had no meaning.

Strong hands angled her hips, preparing her to receive
him. Tara could feel her moist readiness, and so could
he.

*What's happening? How can we read each other's
minds?*

For an instant, she drew back, afraid of what she was
experiencing. Could this be a hallucination, or had they
tapped into a subconscious river that flowed between
them? But surely such things didn't exist.

The Magician paused, watching her. Sensing her confusion and allowing her to sort it out. He would withdraw
if she wished. He had been swept away as much as she,
Tara knew, still hearing the echo of his thoughts, but he
would never pressure her.

As she pulled herself achingly from his mind, she became more aware of him as a man. Muscular, taut, grace-
ful even in the slightest movement. An herbal fragrance

mingled with the faint scent of his exertion. Most remarkable were his eyes, gleaming in the shadowed planes of his face, alive with speculation.

Like a sleek wild hunter he crouched over her, withholding his power. They were separate, but entwined so intimately that with one stroke his body would enter hers.

The self-protective screens that Tara had built around her heart vaporized. They must be united. They belonged together, as one being. Tonight was the only moment that existed, or ever would.

"Yes," she whispered.

His shaft entered her slowly. As the rightness of their joining reverberated through her, Tara felt every centimeter of the man growing with excitement. Something beyond magic was about to happen.

He plunged deep into her. A cry issued from his throat and his back arched.

Pleasure shot through Tara. His rhythmic thrusting lifted her into another sphere, where time passed in tiny flicks of sensation. They were made not of flesh but of light, glimmering and flowing. All the colors of ecstasy merged as he drove into her.

Her breasts registered the demanding pressure of his chest. Her mouth met his again, and then something new rose from the depths of her soul like a great shout of joy.

THE MOON WAS FADING as Chance Powers walked back up the driveway to his house. He stared at the castle facade with distaste. Like his odd name, tonight's set decorations had been bestowed upon him by his father, who had an ulterior motive.

At the door, he ordered the computer to turn off the hologram guardians on the porch. Inside, the house lay silent, the guests gone from the courtyard and the tables bare. The mess could wait until his cleaning staff arrived in the morning.

There was a new sense of emptiness now, without his lady. She had fallen into a deep sleep, a side effect of the intensity of their experience. Her girlfriend, puzzled but good-humored, had hung around until Chance carried his lady downstairs and laid her gently in the back of the car.

By now, they must have reached the street. He doubted they would be able to find their way back here again; people rarely could, unless he summoned them.

Already, he missed her mobile face, alive with an intriguing mixture of naiveté and cynicism. And her rumpled, spiky hair, and the way her lips quirked with emotion. He even missed the sometimes abrupt movements as if she had grown six inches overnight and hadn't yet adjusted to her body.

He yearned to run after the car and bring her back. But it would be a terrible mistake.

It had been his father's idea to throw this Halloween party. Raymond Powers wanted his son to become a partner in the family's multimillion-dollar special-effects business, in which Chance had worked part-time while earning his MBA.

This lavish display, in the house Chance had purchased with his more than generous salary, had been an attempt to seduce him into the good life. If only his father valued his business acumen, instead of the hidden talents that could make them unimaginably rich and powerful.

Their eccentric family had always possessed unusual talents, including the ability to levitate small objects. Raymond also had a touch of ESP with which he tried to second-guess business rivals. Fortunately, from Chance's point of view, it had not proved very reliable.

Raymond had deliberately married a distant cousin in the hope of concentrating their abilities in a child. However, when his abilities began to develop during his teen years, Chance had recognized that it would be wrong to use them for personal gain. For years, he had kept his gifts a secret, even from his parents.

Sometimes he had wondered if he were being selfish. The ability to touch people's minds offered great potential for helping others. Once, by taking some of a friend's pain on himself, he had helped the man recover from the trauma of a motorcycle accident.

He was able not only to read others' thoughts but to influence them. That was the dangerous part. If such powers were misused, they could result in great evil.

Chance might have gone on keeping his father in the dark had it not been for an incident the previous month. He and Raymond had been driving back to their office from a studio where they were consulting on a film. As a traffic light changed, a tiny girl waiting on the sidewalk had pulled away from her mother and run into the path of a truck.

Seeing her danger, the child froze. There was no time for anyone to reach her, and the truck couldn't stop in time.

With a wrenching groan, Chance had flung himself into the girl's mind. With little practice in exercising his talents, he hadn't been sure it would work, but it had. Propelled by his internal command, she'd thrown herself aside just as the truck roared past with brakes squealing.

Exhausted, Chance had returned to himself in time to see the gleam of recognition on his father's face. Now Raymond was full of plans.

The sky was the limit, he declared. Once Chance put to work his skills at mind control, they could dominate their industry, expand into other businesses and even influence legislation. The world would be theirs.

Wearily, Chance gazed around the courtyard. He loved this house, and he knew it would be difficult to afford the payments through honest work.

But tonight something unexpected had happened. He still wasn't quite sure how it had come about.

He hadn't meant to manipulate that delightful sprite into his bed. Entering her mind had been unintentional. In fact, he had the peculiar sense that she had entered his first, but how could that be?

The responsibility lay on his shoulders. Without meaning to, he had taken advantage of a very special lady. He must learn to rein in his powers; already, they had become dangerously strong. Tonight, they had overwhelmed him.

Until now, Chance had weighed the possibility of indulging his father a little without going beyond the bounds of fair play. But this ability to enter others' minds was more potent than he had expected.

He must cut his ties to his family and find his own way in the world. While earning a masters' degree in business, he had discovered an affinity for the financial markets. He must develop his talents in that direction— without using magic.

At the memory of the woman's heightened sensitivity, Chance's body stiffened. He wanted her again, physically and mentally. He wanted to probe what had happened between them, and make sure she hadn't been harmed by it.

But if he'd lost control once around her, it might happen again. At this point in his life, with his abilities coming into full strength while he yet lacked the skill to control them, he might injure her.

At least she shouldn't suffer any great distress from tonight's encounter. What had occurred had been at so deep a level of consciousness that he doubted she would remember it.

But, to be on the safe side, Chance had instinctively acted to protect his privacy by leaving a kind of post-hypnotic suggestion. As far as his lady was concerned, he would be less than a phantom, scarcely a shadow of a memory.

She would go on with her life, only vaguely aware of a sensual experience that would seem more dreamlike than real. She would forget him, and perhaps that was for the best.

But he would never forget her. And he doubted he would ever stop wanting her, either.

Chapter One

Being in the first grade was mostly fun, especially in Mrs. Wilson's classroom, because she kept a chinchilla and two hamsters in cages. Also she read funny stories aloud and let you watch *Winnie the Pooh* cartoons during recess when it rained.

But Harry Blayne hated lunch. He didn't actually hate *his* lunch, because Mommy put good things in it, like granola bars, and celery sticks stuffed with peanut butter, and blue-colored juice. But he hated lunch because John Abernathy the Third always sat at his table.

John Abernathy made fun of the fact that Harry didn't have a daddy. John had *two* daddies, one for weekends and one during the week.

Also, John was a lot bigger because he had repeated kindergarten, and he could make a peashooter out of his straw and whap Harry with it so Harry nearly choked on his granola bar. The teachers never saw John do it, either.

Today was even worse, because it was Friday and the cafeteria was serving pizza. Harry was stuck with his usual lunch because Mommy didn't earn much as an office manager, so he always had to brown-bag it.

John had bullied an extra piece from the little girl next to him. Now, while the lunch monitor was on the other side of the room, he leaned across the table to pester Harry.

"Well, look at Scary Harry!" teased the bully. "Don't you like pizza? I've got two pieces. Bet you wish you had one!"

"Choke on it," muttered Harry.

"Would you like one?" taunted John, holding out a slice of pizza with two tempting circles of pepperoni on it. "Come and get it, Mr. Stupid!" Some of the other kids laughed nervously.

"I don't like pizza," said Harry, even though he wasn't supposed to lie.

John waved the slice so the smell made Harry's stomach rumble. "Well, that's good. I *love* pizza. Did I tell you my daddy buys me a whole pizza anytime I want?"

It wasn't fair. Harry could smell the rich sauce and almost taste the thick cheese. The worst part was that any minute John was going to stick that delicious thing in his mouth.

Then Harry got an idea. It was something he'd been playing with in their apartment, but it upset Mommy, so he only did it in his room now.

He stared at the slice. It quivered, just a tad. John was grinning. "Boy, you really want it, don't you? Maybe you could trade me something for it. How about that new watch you got for your birth—"

With a faint whoosh, the pizza flew through the air, right into Harry's hand. He stuffed it in his mouth before John could grab it back.

A flurry of childish voices could be heard. "Wow!" "Did you see that?" "What happened?" "Harry made the pizza fly!"

"You stole my pizza!" roared John.

"It likes me better than you," said Harry, or that's

what he tried to say, but with his mouth full, it came out a mumble.

"Thief!" John picked up a fork and, to the collective gasp of the watching students, flung it at Harry.

There wasn't time to think or duck. Harry could feel his mind reaching out, very calmly, as if everything had slowed down, and this invisible hand grabbed the fork and heaved it back the way it had come.

John's shriek silenced the cafeteria. A red mark on his forehead showed where the fork had hit.

A fifth-grade teacher stood in the aisle staring at Harry. With a gulp, he realized that she'd seen him make the fork turn around in midair.

Mommy was going to be really, really mad.

TARA PUSHED OPEN the door to her apartment and staggered inside. She hadn't realized there was so much personal stuff in her desk at work until she had to clean it out.

The bright light of midday washed across the living room, picking out every ugly detail of the stained carpet and the threadbare couch. This wasn't the kind of place where she'd imagined herself living and raising a child. Now she was unsure she would even be able to keep this.

Downsizing. Rightsizing. No matter what they called it, the result was that after six years as an office manager, Tara Blayne, single mother, was out of a job.

She dumped the armful of notebooks and desk accessories onto the scarred coffee table. She couldn't turn to her father, who had refused to accept her phone calls or respond to her letters all these years since she decided not to put Harry up for adoption.

Tears threatened to wreck Tara's composure, but she rubbed her eyes fiercely. This wasn't the end of the world. It was just one more setback. At least she had her son, the most precious part of her life.

Maybe she should have listened to Denise and tried to find the father after she discovered she was pregnant. He'd been rich, Denise had pointed out. He ought to help support his own child.

But Tara couldn't bring herself to do it. For one thing, after they discovered they'd misread the street sign and landed at the wrong party, she'd been overwhelmed by a sense of shame at her behavior.

Plus she had such a vague recollection of the man that sometimes she wondered if she'd been drugged. Of course, there was no way of proving that now. But he must have been a terrible person to take advantage of her that way.

And if he *was* rich, that meant he could afford the best lawyers. These days, plenty of men sought custody and got it.

The sharp buzz of the phone startled her. Who would be calling in the middle of the day, when no one was supposed to be home?

"Mrs. Blayne?" came the voice of the school secretary. "I tried your office but they said you'd left. The principal has requested that you come to his office right away. I'm afraid there's been a discipline problem with Harry."

When she related, with apologies for the implausibility, what had happened in the lunchroom, Tara felt a jolt of dismay. She'd tried to tell herself that what she'd seen Harry do with his toys had been a misperception. But now a teacher had witnessed the same thing.

Either the world was going crazy, or Harry's father had been a lot stranger than Tara imagined.

IT WAS NEARLY EIGHT o'clock by the time Chance got home from the office, and he still needed to put in a couple of hours on the computer.

As he crossed the driveway from the garage, his steps crushed some alyssum that had infiltrated the cracks, filling the spring air with the flowers' honeyed essence. Involuntarily, he imagined his lady beside him and how she would relish the gentle fragrance. But she was only a ghost of a memory, elusive as a moonbeam.

At his approach, colored floodlights bathed the front of the house. The stucco had been painted last year, an earthy tan, and the trim redone in chocolate.

As his financial consulting firm prospered, Chance should have redecorated long ago, but something had stopped him. The ugly marks left by the castle facade had served as a reminder of the Halloween that had been the turning point in his life.

Everything that had happened since had come from the lessons he learned that night. Even when the paint deteriorated into an eyesore, it had been hard to give up the last tangible reminder of that night.

Every once in a while, over the past seven years, Chance had felt the urge to track the lady down. But even now, he wasn't sure he might not somehow harm her if they met again.

He had struggled to gain control over his abilities, but there were no classes in how to keep from invading other people's minds. So he had found his own way, beginning with meditation and proceeding to a study of Eastern and Native American beliefs.

Gradually he had schooled himself to erect an imaginary glass wall between himself and others whenever temptation beckoned. It worked, but it made him feel shut off, as if he were wearing gloves when he yearned to touch the surface of the world.

His father still believed Chance's success as an investment adviser and stockbroker must come from trickery. Sadly, the man couldn't understand his son's attachment to ethics.

Some things, Chance supposed as he mounted the front porch, never changed. He loved his father, but he doubted he and Ray would ever be on the same wavelength.

To the computer, he said, "Today's password is...ketchup."

"Wrong," it said in a dry, nasal tone.

"Oh, shoot. That was yesterday." Chance wished he could make the thing recognize his voice. He supposed he could carry a remote control, but then he had to worry about losing the darn thing. "It's mustard." He was working his way through the condiments this week.

As the lock released its grip, a deep sigh arose from the house. "You're late again. I don't suppose you've eaten dinner, have you?" Its whiny voice lay in the high-tenor range.

"No. What've we got?"

After an almost infinitesimal pause, the computer said, "Tuna salad. Curried rice. Yogurt, assorted flavors. You ought to eat the rest of that fried chicken you brought home yesterday. As you know, Rajeev's a vegetarian."

"Thank you for your concern." Shouldering his way through the door, Chance wondered what perverse impulse had led him to design a computer program that nagged.

As he entered the living room, wall sconces bloomed with light. The voluptuousness of the velour couches, lacquered chests and Persian carpets struck him as gaudy, but he never spent time in this room anyway. His housekeeper had to clean the darn things, so Chance had allowed Rajeev and his sister, who also lived on the premises, to pick the furnishings.

Turning to his right, he wandered down a hall to the kitchen. Shining butcher-block counters, freshly waxed linoleum and gleaming stainless-steel sinks testified to Rajeev's efficiency. Prompted by the computer, the toaster oven was preheating.

Chance peered into the refrigerator. Using his mind, he shifted a few items until he could retrieve the chicken. Levitating objects might be a mere parlor trick, but it was good for mental discipline.

After putting the chicken in the oven, he ambled down the hall to his bedroom suite. He'd always slept in the tower until that night with his lady, but since then it had brought back too many vivid memories.

He needed to forget the woman and move on. Chance aroused plenty of feminine interest in the course of his work. Why couldn't he bring himself to return any of it?

As he unknotted his tie, the sudden blare of recorded music stunned him into nearly strangling himself. After the initial startled moment, his senses identified a sultry tango.

Slipping into jeans and a polo shirt, Chance adjourned to the courtyard. There, beneath spotlights, two exotic figures tormented each other across the flagstones. A man's shiny shoe stamped out a beat, a multicolored skirt snapped and a lithe female body twirled as two pairs of black eyes met and defied each other.

"Extension!"

"Hand position!"

"Tilt your head!"

"Too slow, too slow!"

The words rasped in time to the music. Sweat beaded

on dark skin. Faster, faster they pounded, until the dancers flung themselves into a back-bending, arm-bracing finale.

"Well?" said Rajeev, pushing his sister unceremoniously to her feet. "What do you think, eh?"

"Better," Chance decided. "You're definitely getting the hang of it."

"But do you think we have any hope of a trophy?" asked Vareena, smoothing her skirt. Although five inches shorter than her brother, she had the same dramatic coloring and erect posture.

Three years ago—a year after Rajeev came to work for Chance—the pair had fallen in love with dancing while watching the movie *Strictly Ballroom*. A clerk at a convenience store, Vareena practiced with her brother whenever possible. Now the waltz, the paso doble, the tango and the samba echoed through Chance's dreams.

"As much hope as anyone," he said. "Great costumes, except..." He changed the color of Vareena's hair ribbon from green to a shimmering rainbow. "Think you could find a fabric like that?"

"Truly wonderful," said Rajeev.

Vareena removed the ribbon and studied it. "Yes, yes, very nice. I will look for it."

Chance relaxed his concentration, and the green color returned. The brother and sister applauded. They never lost their appreciation of his antics.

On the way back to the kitchen, he wondered why he had ever thought hiring a housekeeper of Indian descent would complement his interest in meditation. Anything even faintly mystical bored Rajeev to tears.

The tantalizing scent of fried chicken made his stomach rumble as he fixed a plate of food. Grabbing a can of soda, Chance moved down the hall to his master suite, where he had equipped the front den with a laserdisc player, a big-screen TV and a Pentium computer with CD-ROM and a huge selection of games.

Dropping onto the couch, he flicked the TV to the local news. What followed was the usual jumble of car chases, picketers, politics and weather. He was about to switch it off and retreat to his home office when the announcer's words arrested him.

"Now for a tale of black magic, or white magic, in a most unlikely setting! Find out where, when we come back."

It was probably a story about a psychic fair, Chance supposed, but he needed to find out. The Powers family was unusual in its gifts, but not unique. If someone with real ability was giving a demonstration, he wanted to know about it.

Most people, of course, would do almost anything to keep such talents secret. If you didn't, people dismissed you as a kook. Chance's cousin Merton had nearly derailed his accounting career by getting drunk at a party and literally juggling some books—hands-free.

If one person had been born with the ability to read minds, it could happen again. The next recipient might not be so honest, either.

The commercials ended and a microphone-wielding reporter posed in front of a low building. "Two first graders were suspended from Palm Mesa Elementary School earlier today after one of them allegedly threw a fork at the other. School officials claim the intended target mentally flipped the fork in midair and made it strike the first child."

A beefy woman appeared on camera, holding a boy who looked large for a first grader. His forehead sported a purple bruise.

"Suspending my son is unfair, and that's why I called the press!" bellowed the mother. "How dare they say Johnny threw the fork, when he's obviously the victim! Nobody with any brains believes in magic! What are they teaching our children, anyway?"

"A teacher claims she saw the fork change course in the air, but did she?" the reporter asked the camera. "The teacher refused to speak on camera, but let's talk to the other mom."

The picture cut to a tall, slender woman trying to steer a boy down the front steps. Chance's breath caught in his throat.

It was his lady. There was no mistaking the short, willful brown hair or those wide-set olive eyes.

"Mrs. Blayne?" asked the announcer, and Chance's heart sank. Apparently she was married. But then, wasn't that obvious, since she had a child?

"Yes?" Her troubled gaze met the camera.

"What do you think of the claim that your son has mental powers?"

"Harry's a normal kid," she snapped, shielding the small, dark-haired figure from the camera. "He probably stuck his hand up and batted the fork back."

"Do you think he should have been suspended?"

Maternal fury flashed from the TV screen. "For defending himself? Absolutely not! Now, please excuse us. I think everyone is making too much of this."

As she led the little boy away, he glanced back, and for the first time Chance saw the child's face. It was small and impish, not unlike the mother's, except for his eyes.

They had a slight, exotic tilt. As the TV lights reflected into them, they appeared for an instant to turn silver.

Chance sat bolt upright. Impossible. Unthinkable. Without weighing the consequences, he forced the camera filming the episode to rewind and play again in slow motion.

This time, the effect was unmistakable. The child looked up, the lights glimmered, the eyes turned silver. There was no mistaking the resemblance to Chance.

From the TV, an offscreen voice said, "I'm sorry, we seem to be experiencing some technical difficulties."

With a start, he released the camera, and watched the lady of his dreams hurry down the steps with his son. There was still a slightly coltish air to her, an appealing youthfulness despite what she must have gone through these past several years.

She'd borne him a son. Regret and guilt lumped inside Chance's stomach. It had never occurred to him that his lady might be pregnant.

Had she tried to find him? He doubted it, knowing that her memories of that evening must be blurred. Besides, Chance was hardly a reclusive figure in Los Angeles, even guesting on local talk shows to provide expert commentary about changes in the stock market. It was possible the lady had seen him and not even recognized the father of her son.

Mrs. Blayne. Or Ms. Blayne, more likely. At least he knew her name, or part of it. Not that he needed to. Now that he had learned of the existence of a son, Chance would have no trouble finding either of them.

And find them he must. The boy was headed for trouble if he didn't learn to harness his abilities. Heaven knew what the future held, if he was already showing talent so early. Usually it didn't develop until adolescence.

There was an even greater danger: that Raymond Powers, or someone like him, would see this newscast and recognize the boy's potential. Chance doubted that Ms.

Blayne, despite her maternal fierceness, would be able to protect her son against such sophisticated exploiters.

Anxiously, he flipped from channel to channel, but if any other newscast aired a similar segment, he didn't see it. This time, the boy might have escaped Ray's notice, although Chance's unthinking trick of replaying the tape had certainly pointed a finger.

For one soul-searching moment, he forced himself to consider whether his motives might be selfish. The sight of Ms. Blayne had aroused a pervasive sensual awareness and a deep-rooted yearning to see her again. Furthermore, in Chance's family, the greatest powers were inherited by the firstborn. Any subsequent children might be gifted, but none so much as—as—Harry, wasn't that his son's name?

This was going to be a tricky business. Ethics required Chance to tell the woman the truth, but he doubted she would believe him. If he put matters too bluntly, she was likely to flee in alarm, perhaps even get a court order keeping him away.

He would have to be subtle. He would have to guide Ms. Blayne until she reached the point where she could absorb the truth.

Chapter Two

"Something's got to turn up soon." Denise transferred a
third slice of pepperoni pizza onto Harry's plate. They
were sitting on Tara's living room floor on a blanket,
having an impromptu substitute for the picnic that had
just been rained out.

"You'd think so, wouldn't you?" Tara hated to give
in to negative feelings, especially in front of her son. But
the rent was due soon and her two weeks of job searching
had led nowhere.

Her son, newly reinstated in school, began regaling
Denise with stories of his rivalry with the class bully. A
couple of times he stopped himself in midsentence, and
Tara suspected the boy was hiding something.

She had a good idea what it must be. She'd forbidden
Harry to use his tricks, but he was probably doing it when
he didn't think any adults could see. In a way, she was
glad it was spring vacation so she could keep a closer
eye on him.

Surely he wasn't *really* doing magic. He had to be
faking it in some clever way. If she weren't so stressed-
out about unemployment, she would have gotten to the
bottom of this by now.

Outside, rain pelted the window. The downpour suited her mood.

Government economists kept announcing that new jobs were being created by the bushel. Maybe so, but job seekers must be springing up even faster, because everywhere Tara applied, she found herself in a long line of applicants.

There had been two offers, but one involved a beginner's salary too low to support her son, and the other required working weekends and nights. If she had a family to help her, maybe she could have managed such a difficult schedule, but Tara was alone.

On Saturday, she'd broken down and called her father in Louisville to ask if he would help her find a job there. A bank executive, he might know of openings for which Tara was qualified. All she asked was information and a place to stay while she sought work.

Through some cousins, she knew that her father had remarried a woman with a teenage daughter. They owned a large house with guest quarters.

He had coldly informed Tara that he considered her and her illegitimate child a bad example for his stepdaughter. As far as he was concerned, her problems were her own fault.

This icy rejection, after her attempt to patch years of estrangement, was the final straw. Tara would never turn to him again.

For one brief moment, she measured what her life might have been had she not become pregnant. She would have earned a business degree, perhaps qualified for an executive position and put in the long hours necessary for advancement. By now, at age twenty-nine, she ought to be earning a healthy salary.

Then her gaze alit on Harry, his face gleeful as he told

Denise how he'd won the first-grade spelling bee last week and earned an ice-cream party for his class. Even the bully had been grateful.

What was the point in trying to imagine life without him? From the moment she'd learned she was pregnant, Tara had known her life would revolve around her child.

But being a responsible parent meant providing for him. This afternoon, while he played, she would answer the ads she'd circled in the newspaper this morning. Denise had been a great sport, offering to take Harry to the beauty shop with her whenever Tara landed an interview.

The ringing of the phone startled her. Whenever she heard it, Tara couldn't help leaping to her feet and running to answer, hoping it might be a job offer.

"Hello?" She hoped she didn't sound out of breath. "I mean, this is Tara Blayne."

"Ms. Blayne? Chance Powers here." The caller had a rich baritone voice, commanding but gentle as it vibrated across the phone lines. "President of Powers Financial Corporation. You responded to my ad for a personal assistant. Are you still available?"

"Yes. Yes, I am."

She didn't remember applying to Powers Financial Corporation, but she had sent several résumés in response to "blind" ads that simply listed post office boxes. She did recognize the name of his company, which was known for its expertise in investments.

With her experience managing an office, she would have preferred a higher position than that of personal assistant. However, if it paid decently and offered benefits, she'd be glad to get it.

Also, she'd heard Chance Powers referred to as the "Wall Street Wizard of the West." It would be intriguing to work for someone so dynamic.

"I was wondering if you were free this afternoon for an interview. Unless the rain poses a problem, of course." He sounded almost nervous, but then, some people hated conducting interviews.

Actually, the timing was perfect, since Denise had Mondays off and could stay with Harry. "Today would be fine. Is there any further information you need about me?"

"If you could bring another copy of your résumé, that would help," the man said. "My secretary seems to have misplaced the one you sent."

They set the time at 3:00 p.m. and he gave her directions. After she hung up, Tara had the inexplicable sense that more had transpired between them than a phone conversation about employment. But that must be a result of her anxiety.

CHANCE STARED at the clock on the wall. Slowly the hands edged toward 3:00. Annoyed, he returned them to the 2:45 position.

There were definite disadvantages to being able to move objects, particularly when you didn't intend to. It was too bad his abilities didn't extend to speeding time itself.

After seeing Tara on television, he'd tracked her easily through the computer. His impulse was to contact her at once, but when he learned of her layoff, he realized it offered a perfect opportunity.

Eager as he was to get close to Harry, Chance needed to proceed slowly enough to win Tara's trust. Only then would she allow him to help guide the boy's future.

Besides, what would he say? *Hi, I'm the man who seduced and abandoned you. Sorry I didn't know about the kid, but here I am, so let's share custody.* Yeah, right.

Chance had laid the groundwork. He'd announced to his staff that he needed help outside normal business hours, which was true. Besides, working weekends and evenings together would require Tara to spend time at his home office, and he planned to invite her to bring her son along.

Then he'd placed a blind ad. She hadn't responded, but he doubted she would realize that. He'd had to finesse the part about losing her résumé, but she'd bought it.

It was sheer good luck that she hadn't found another position during the past two weeks, but the sluggish economy had worked in Chance's favor. Now he just had to persuade her to take the position.

"Mr. Powers?" came his secretary's voice on the intercom. "Miss Blayne is here."

Rushing out to greet her might look suspicious. It would also make his secretary suspect he'd taken leave of his senses. With forced calmness, Chance said, "Send her in."

Then he assumed an air of detachment and stood to greet the newcomer.

POWERS FINANCIAL Corporation occupied a low-key, palm-shaded building along a side street in Beverly Hills. From the moment she stepped into its flower-filled entryway, Tara felt at home.

Pausing in front of a mirrored wall, she straightened the skirt of her rose-colored suit. The high collar of the tan blouse flattered her long neck, and, with more than a little help from Denise, her hair was behaving itself for a change.

She felt ready to go back to work, and this would be an ideal environment. Now if only Mr. Chance Powers didn't turn out to be an ogre.

After an elevator ride to the second story, Tara pushed aside the double glass doors bearing the name of the firm. A receptionist directed her to an office suite, where the secretary buzzed her boss.

Tara wondered where a personal assistant would fit in, and what her duties might be. Was the man seeking a potential executive or did he want a coffeemaker and gofer?

She braced herself for whatever might come. There would be other job possibilities, she told herself. But whether it was because Mr. Powers himself had called her or due to the pleasantness of the surroundings, this one felt right.

"Go on in," said the secretary.

"Thanks." Fighting the instinct to check her hand mirror one last time, Tara stepped through the inner door.

Her first impression was of vast space, soothing light and gleaming wooden surfaces, but this was merely the setting. Behind a large desk stood a figure who dominated the room.

What was it about the man that gave him such an aura of authority? He was tall and muscular, his dark hair slightly overgrown. A suppleness in his gray suit hinted of silk, but there was nothing soft about the planes of his face.

"I'm Tara Blayne." Crossing the room, she thrust out her hand, and found it seized in a firm grip. As they touched, a sense of dislocation came over her, and for one disconcerting moment she imagined she could see herself from his perspective: skin flushed, tan blouse drawn snugly across her breasts, lips slightly parted.

Then, as if a door had slammed shut, the connection broke. At his gesture to be seated, Tara chose a hard-

backed chair, barely remembering to place the copy of
her résumé on his desk before she sat.

What was wrong with her? She didn't usually respond
to men this way, especially not in an employment situation. In fact, she had found men uninteresting these past
years since she'd become a mother. Further, she knew
that allowing any hint of sexuality in an office relationship was flirting with danger.

Chance Powers settled back, regarding her dubiously.
At least, she guessed that doubts might be what caused
the coldness in his expression. She wondered if he had
guessed her response and was offended.

She decided to seize the initiative. "As you can see, I
have six years of office experience, including managerial
background. I've studied accounting, and my computer
skills are up-to-date."

"Know anything about the stock market?" he asked.

There hadn't been time to brush up since his phone
call a few hours earlier. "Not much," Tara admitted.

"Good." The Wall Street Wizard leaned forward, elbows on the desk. His eyes had a faint slant that struck
her as familiar, until she realized that he looked a little
like her son. The similarity was disturbing, and she thrust
it from her mind. "I have my own way of analyzing and
forecasting trends. I prefer not to be hampered by pre-
conceived ideas."

"Could you provide me with a specific job description?" Tara wanted to be as forthright as possible. It
helped keep her from getting intimidated, and, judging
by his brisk way of speaking, the man was accustomed
to directness. "A personal assistant could be almost anything."

His speculative look caught her by surprise. She had

the impression he was trying to figure out what to say to win her over, but why would he do that?

"Frankly, it's the first time I've employed anyone in this capacity, so I'm still defining the job duties," he said at last. "Running a company like this requires putting in long hours. I have to keep tabs on developments all over the world, and the world never sleeps."

A knot formed in Tara's stomach. She hoped this wasn't going to be another job that required working evenings and weekends, but it sure sounded like it.

"My regular employees aren't always available when I need them," Powers went on, watching her closely. "Also, sometimes I'll start a project in the off-hours, which spills over into the regular work week. It wastes time if I have to start someone from scratch. I need an assistant who can be available on a flexible basis. With a full-time salary, of course."

The knot in her stomach tightened. "Mr. Powers, I'd love to work for you and I'd love to learn more about the financial field. But I'm a single mother. There's no one to watch my son at odd hours."

Picking up her résumé, he glanced over it. Was he looking for some mention of a child? Tara hadn't cited her parental status, suspecting that some employers might be deterred.

"The truth is, in some ways you're overqualified for the position," he said.

She had heard those words before, with variations. Overqualified, overexperienced, too high a salary. Why couldn't employers understand that she was willing to take a step backward if she had to?

"I'm willing to start lower down the ladder if it's with the right company," she said. "I could arrange to work *some* off-hours. It's just...well, finding baby-sitters isn't easy. And I hate to leave my son with anyone I don't know well.''

His mouth tightened and he glanced away. Tara caught the impression that her words had somehow made him feel guilty. Perhaps he hated to turn down a single mother because she needed the job so badly.

''As I said, I'm still working out the details of this position.'' When the man folded his hands in front of him, the knuckles gleamed white. He *was* tense, but why? ''I need someone absolutely reliable, who will be discreet about my clients' information and who comes with the highest recommendation. Someone, in short, who's over-qualified to be a personal assistant. You fit that description better than anyone else who answered our ad.''

Tara pressed her lips together, confused. Her résumé cited references on request, so he hadn't seen them. How could he know she came with the highest recommendation? But then, she reflected, he could have called her former boss.

''I wish I knew how to resolve this problem with the hours,'' she said. ''My girlfriend is willing to baby-sit occasionally, but—''

''If you're willing, you could do some of the work at your apartment,'' Chance said. ''Or bring your son to my house—'' He paused as if mulling an idea. ''You know, it might work.''

''What might?''

''It occurs to me,'' he said, ''that the best solution might be for you and your son to move into my house.''

Why would he want them to live with him? Was he expecting her to serve as a maid? ''I'm not sure what you mean,'' she said.

He smiled with a trace of embarrassment. The expression softened his face and hinted at another, more approachable side to him.

With a jolt, Tara realized what she'd been denying ever since she walked into this room. She was attracted to Mr. Chance Powers. It was more than mere attraction; all her senses had become heightened as if she were receiving signals from him at a subliminal level.

A few minutes ago, a door had seemed to shut between them, but gradually it had swung open again. She could feel his awareness sweep over and through her, touching the most private places. Without realizing it, she had become so aroused that if he were to sweep her into his arms at this moment, she would be ready for him.

Heat flooded Tara's face. How could this be happening again? Nearly seven years ago she'd made the same kind of mistake, and thrown her life in an unexpected direction.

She didn't need any more left turns into the unknown. She needed a job, and she wasn't going to ruin her opportunity by letting Chance know how he affected her.

"I suppose moving into my home would be unusual," he said. "But, like a lot of people in my position, I maintain a home office that functions twenty-four hours a day."

"I'm afraid I *don't* function twenty-four hours a day," she retorted with more tartness than she'd intended.

He broke into a laugh. "I'm afraid I've given you the wrong idea. First of all, Ms. Blayne, the way my house is laid out, you and your son would have a private suite. Your own apartment, as it were. Your free time would be your own."

She hated to admit how appealing that sounded. The high cost of rent in Los Angeles was eating her budget alive. Furthermore, she would love to transfer Harry to a different school, away from his fork-flinging nemesis.

Living in the same house with a sexy man could present problems. Yet since that moment when she'd felt a wave of desire, the vibrations between them had ebbed again. Surely she could keep her feelings under control, or perhaps they would disappear entirely with time.

"In addition," the man went on, "I have a full-time housekeeper. He handles the routine cooking and cleaning, and he could watch your son when you're busy."

The possibility of finding a live-in position had never occurred to Tara, since her skills lay in office work. But the advantages were obvious. With Harry in the same house, she could work evenings while he slept.

"What about travel?" she asked.

"I go to New York and Tokyo occasionally," Chance said, "but not very often. And I might not need you to come with me. If I ever did, my housekeeper and his sister live on the premises, so between them, Ha—your son would be well looked after."

Something was wrong here. Tara couldn't imagine why this man would make inquiries about her son, but apparently he had. "Did you start to say 'Harry'?"

"Harry?" Chance blinked, a touch too quickly. "Who's—? Oh! Your son."

"How did you know his name?" Tara pressed.

He studied her thoughtfully. She felt a tickle between her ears, as if the man were probing her mind and replaying her thoughts like a videotape. Searching for an explanation, some way to cover his blunder.

What blunder? Why am I so suspicious of him? What could he possibly be hiding?

Then he nodded with what she could have sworn was relief. "Sorry, but I realized that I *did* know his name and I was trying to remember how. I called your former employer for a recommendation, and he must have mentioned the boy. Harry. Is he named after someone in your family?"

It was a reasonable explanation, and the man seemed on the verge of offering her the job. Tara hoped she wasn't turning into one of those foolish people who mistrust good fortune so much that they destroy it.

"It's kind of silly," she said. "You see, even though it was my first birth, Harry came out with almost no labor pains. If my waters hadn't broken first, I don't think I'd have had enough warning to make it to the hospital in time."

It seemed like an inappropriate detail to reveal at a job interview, but Chance showed no reaction, so she went on. "My girlfriend, who was my labor coach, suggested I name him after Harry Houdini because he appeared as if by magic. So I did."

Tara had intended to name the boy Andrew, after her father. But when she called him from the hospital and he spoke only words of condemnation, she had seized on Denise's suggestion.

"I've heard of that before," Chance said. "That painless labor."

"Even for a first-time mom?" The nurses at the hospital had been amazed. "Really?"

"It runs in certain families. Or so I've heard," he said. "Well, when can you start?"

He was offering her the job! It was almost too good to be true, but Tara refused to yield to her doubts. The rent was due next week, so the sooner she moved out, the better. "How about Monday?"

"You can settle in over the weekend," said her new boss, writing down directions to his house. "Will you need any help? I could arrange to put your furniture into storage.''

"It's rented with the apartment," Tara said. "I can manage the rest of the stuff myself. Thanks, Mr. Powers. I promise I'll do my best."

"Do your best to call me Chance, will you?" he said.

"Certainly, Chance." They shook hands and then, her head whirling, Tara marched toward the door.

It was hard to absorb that she was no longer unemployed. Then, realizing that he hadn't mentioned a salary, she paused. Would it be better to ask now or call later?

"The salary," he said as if reading her thoughts, "is fifty dollars more per week than your old job."

"That would be fine." She would get a raise *and* a free place to live? At this rate, she should finally be able to put aside some savings!

Whatever doubts she might have about moving in with a stranger were pushed aside. In Los Angeles, lots of important people worked at home and employed staff there. Movie stars, for instance.

A financial adviser was hardly a movie star. But Tara had no intention of second-guessing her stroke of luck. She intended to spend the rest of spring vacation celebrating with her son.

THAT HAD BEEN a close call. Chance couldn't believe his carelessness in revealing that he knew Harry's name.

The entire interview had been a test of his self-control. The moment Tara walked in, he'd felt himself drawn into her mind the way he had that night at his party. That had been a strange sensation, viewing his own office through someone else's eyes.

Not just his office but himself. Chance Powers, financial hotshot, big and imperious, holding the reins of power.

He didn't want to control Tara or anyone else. If he were the sort of man who enjoyed manipulating others, he would have gone along with his father's schemes.

Yet he *had* maneuvered her into moving in with him, and thank goodness for it. To have Harry living with him would mean plenty of opportunities to observe the child and influence him. And the boy would be much safer at Chance's house than living alone with an overworked single mom.

But there were other dangers created by the situation, Chance reflected, leaning back in his chair and steepling his fingers. If he'd had this much difficulty holding himself apart from Tara during the interview, with at least one lapse, what would happen when they found themselves together night after night?

For him, the most difficult part of the interview had come when she described Harry's birth. He should have been there. She shouldn't have had to rely on a girlfriend, no matter how loyal. And Chance would give almost anything to have watched his son emerge into the light, and to hold the newborn infant in his arms.

Birth with little pain was a much-appreciated characteristic of the Powers family. The greater the magic talents, the easier the child's delivery into this world. Harry Houdini, indeed.

This son of his must be one unusual kid, Chance reflected. He couldn't wait to meet the little guy.

Chapter Three

Tara was glad she had her new job to look forward to, because during these past few days it seemed as if everything that could go wrong had gone wrong.

The landlady refused to refund the security deposit and last month's rent because Tara was moving out on such short notice. Tara would have agreed except that she knew the woman had a grown son who wanted to occupy the unit as soon as possible. Finally, on threat of a suit in small-claims court, the landlady agreed to return the rent but not the deposit.

Then Harry fell off his bicycle, scraping his arm and chin and muttering that he didn't think he could chew. Alarmed that he might have broken his jaw, Tara rushed him to the emergency room. He turned out to be only bruised, but the medical bill nearly fractured her bank account.

Finally, when she came out to load the car on Friday afternoon, she discovered that some trickster had let the air out of her tires. The neighborhood abounded with undisciplined kids, and there was no telling which one had sneaked into the carport and done it.

As Tara stood staring at her sunken car and trying to figure out how to remedy the situation, an ice blue sports car whipped into a space along the curb. The man behind the wheel, partially obscured by glare on the windshield, didn't move for a few minutes, and then she saw that he was talking to someone she couldn't see. Tara assumed he had a hands-free cell phone.

From the apartment building, Harry struggled out with his arms full of stuffed animals. As he passed the sports car, he stopped and peered inside.

"Hey, Mom!" he called. "This guy's talking to his car!"

"It's a mobile phone," she said. "Come on, Harry, give the man a little space." Hurrying toward her son, she got a better look at the driver and realized it was Chance Powers.

It was kind of him to help them move, since that was the only explanation she could think of for his presence. But how embarrassing to saddle him with the problem of how to revive her droopy tires!

"No, no," said the boy. "He's really talking to the car!"

At that moment, Chance's door popped open without any apparent action on his part. Sunlight played across his thick dark hair, raising russet highlights. From this angle, his sculpted cheekbones and straight nose made him resemble a Greek sculpture.

She could smell the herbal fragrance of his shampoo, and feel the moisture on his skin as if he'd showered only moments before. She could see him stepping from the shower, beads of water gleaming on his tanned skin, mouth curving upward as he glanced into the mirror....

With a shock, she yanked her thoughts from the tantalizing image that presented itself. How dare she invade the man's privacy by imagining what he looked like naked. Yet she had the weirdest sense that she *hadn't* been imagining it, but remembering.

"The boy's right," he said, uncoiling from the tight-fitting interior. "We were debating the best way to rein-flate your tires."

"Debating?" Tara knew that men enjoyed buying the latest gadgets, but to her knowledge even the most advanced cars restricted themselves to advising that the hatchback hadn't latched or the gas was low.

"It was hardly a debate," came a sulky female voice from inside the car. "How could anyone believe a bicycle pump would have sufficient pressure to inflate a car tire?"

"The nearest gas station can't be more than a few blocks away," Chance pointed out. "They would only need enough air to—"

"Then there was his other idea!" scoffed the car. "He was going to take off all four tires and pile them inside *me*. Does it look like I'm that kind of car?"

Reaching to the dashboard, Chance pressed a button next to the computerized map. The voice stopped.

"Wow!" Harry gave an excited hop. "That's cool!"

"I'm thinking of reprogramming it to say 'Yes, master,'" muttered Chance, and then brightened. "You must be Harry."

Tara introduced her son to her new boss. Despite her frustration about the tires, she was glad for the amusing distraction. Obviously, life at the Powers residence was going to be full of surprises.

She hoped that being exposed to Chance's computer wizardry would make Harry forget his attempts at feigning magic. The boy was old enough to differentiate between fantasy and reality, and to put his mind to practical use. Having access to the latest technology would be a blessing.

Although she took pride in handling her own life, Tara had to admit that it felt good to have someone to turn to. Especially someone as solid and reassuring as Chance.

"As you can see, we've been the victim of some juvenile delinquent," she said as her boss surveyed the sagging sedan. "Any suggestions? Short of calling a tow truck, I mean?"

"I'll bet I can fix it!" Harry dumped his teddy bears into the back seat and planted himself in front of a tire. "If I concentrate, I can make the air go in. Watch!"

To Tara's horror, the tire began, ever so slowly, to inflate. Or, rather, it appeared to be filling, but the illusion must have been due to the power of suggestion.

"Whoa!" Chance clapped the boy on the back, which had the effect of breaking his concentration. The tire drooped. "You'll bust your gut, blowing so hard!"

"I wasn't blowing," Harry pointed out.

"I'll tell you what, sport." The older man crouched to the height of the little boy. Puzzled, Tara observed that they seemed to resemble each other, not only in the slant of their eyes but also in the shapes of their ears. Then, blinking to clear her vision, she took a closer look and decided the resemblance was superficial. "I'll show you how a real man handles a situation like this, okay?"

Straightening, he took Tara aside. The brush of his hand against her arm nearly overwhelmed her self-control. When they were touching, she felt intimately connected to him in a way she couldn't explain.

Chance's gaze was hooded. "You've probably got a lot to do inside, rounding up the rest of your things. I'll take care of getting help. This will give me a chance to get to know your son. He seems like a bright little boy."

"A little too bright." She knew Chance was going to insist on paying for the repairs himself, but at the moment she couldn't afford to stand on her pride. "Thanks, Mr. Powers."

He quirked an eyebrow.

"Chance," she said. "Thanks, Chance."

"Don't worry about it." He stepped back, admitting Harry to their conversation. "We'll have it taken care of in no time."

HARRY HOPED Mr. Powers wasn't going to make fun of magic. It was getting harder and harder to restrain himself, especially when there were problems that could be fixed so easily and that made so much trouble for his mother.

"Just let me do it, will you?" he told the man.

Chance crouched down again. It was nice to be able to look a grown-up in the face, especially when that face had a friendly expression to it.

"It's not that simple." The man spoke seriously. "Harry, you don't want to let the whole world know what you can do."

"Why not?"

"First of all, they'll think you're tricking them."

That was true, but Harry was tired of worrying about other people's stupidity. "Yeah, but so what? I mean, this is *our* car. Why can't I fix it?"

"You know about bad guys on TV, don't you?"

Mom didn't let him watch violent shows, but there were bad guys in cartoons. "Sure."

"What do you think a bad guy would do if he found out that a little boy could work magic?"

Harry got excited. "He'd make the boy open bank

vaults! And get passwords to people's computers so he could steal their money!''

''But first,'' Chance warned solemnly, ''he'd have to kidnap the little boy, wouldn't he?''

Harry's enthusiasm faded. He didn't want some robber taking him away. ''Yeah. So you mean—'' He swallowed hard. ''Mom's right. I shouldn't do magic stuff.''

''Did I say that?'' Chance shook his head. ''The key, young fellow, is to do your magic so that nobody suspects. The first step is to take a good look around and make sure nobody's watching you.''

Harry felt good again. He'd tried to hide his magic when he was just fooling around, but when Mom needed him, he'd blundered ahead in full view of everyone. What Mr. Powers said made him feel more in control of himself. On the other hand...

''It's not right to keep secrets from Mommy,'' he said.

The man sighed. ''I'm glad your mother's raising you to be honest, and I don't want to change that. But until you get more skilled at doing magic, she isn't going to believe you.''

Was it possible that Mr. Powers meant what Harry thought he did? ''You mean you could help me get better? And then we could show Mom, and she'd stop giving me such a hard time?''

''I hope that's how it will work.''

Harry decided he could trust this new friend, and not just because Mom liked him. There was something about Mr. Powers that seemed familiar, as if Harry knew him already. And he understood about the magic, which nobody else did.

''Okay,'' Harry said. ''What do we do?''

Chance surveyed the carport area and the adjacent street. ''Can anybody see us?''

A delivery truck poked out of a driveway across the street. "He might notice something."

"Then let's wait."

It took several minutes, while a group of kids walked by on the sidewalk and then a lady came outside to empty her trash, before the coast was clear. Harry was afraid Mom would return before they got the job done, but finally Chance gave him the go-ahead.

"Now, here's something to consider," the man said. "If you inflate one tire all the way, what will happen?"

Harry squinted at the car. "It'll be tipped funny."

"And something might get damaged."

"I should take turns, so they all get filled up a little at a time, right?" Harry was proud of himself for figuring it out.

"Right." Mr. Powers reached over and ruffled his hair. It was the kind of fond gesture that John Abernathy's father—the weekend dad who brought him to school on Monday mornings—sometimes used when he said goodbye. It gave Harry a warm, squishy feeling. "Want to try it?"

"Sure." Harry squinted at the tires. This was harder than anything he'd done before, because he had to keep working at it. The car perked up a little but after a few minutes he couldn't push it anymore.

"I guess I'm not good enough," he said.

An eyebrow lifted. "Not good enough? Do you know any other little boys who can put air into tires just by thinking about it?"

That made Harry feel better. "No."

"You need to learn how to focus." A half smile touched the man's face, as if he were remembering something. "I had to work things out for myself. I didn't dare let my father know what I could do because he might make me do too much of it.''

''That doesn't make sense,'' Harry said.

''It will when you're older.'' The man returned his attention to the car. ''What you have to do is to visualize the air going into the tire and puffing it out, one centimeter at a time. You were probably trying to do it all at once, picturing the tire completely back to normal, right?''

''Sort of.'' Harry wasn't sure what he'd been doing. He'd always relied on instinct.

''Patience is required to do anything of substance.'' Chance's face took on an expression as if he were staring at something no one else could see.

Harry got an eerie feeling. He'd never watched anyone else work magic, and he'd never thought about how it would look. Even before anything happened, he could feel power surging through the man. *He's really special.*

Then he forgot everything but the car. Slowly, smoothly, the body began to rise as the tires regained their shape. There was no jerkiness as Mr. Powers transferred his attention from one wheel to another. It was almost as if he could control all four at once, which meant he *really* had this down pat.

''About thirty pounds per square inch ought to do it,'' said Chance, his expression returning to normal.

Before them, the car stood with quiet dignity on its restored tires. Harry went over and patted the bumper. ''Wow,'' he said. ''Will you teach me how to do that?''

''Yes, under two conditions,'' the man said.

Harry gulped. He hoped they weren't anything Mom would disapprove of, because he wanted to learn this stuff more than he'd ever wanted anything, except a father. ''Like what?''

"Number one, nobody outside our household ever sees you do it," Chance said. "No tricks at school. No impressing your friends."

"Okay." That wouldn't be easy, but Harry could handle it.

"And second, you never do anything to hurt or cheat anyone." Mr. Powers wasn't smiling now. "No messing with people's minds or poking into other people's business. You can play games to amuse yourself, or you can help others if it won't attract attention, but that's all."

What a relief. Harry had been worried that maybe this new friend would want him to do something bad, but obviously he didn't. "I swear."

"And in return," Chance said, "I promise to help you become an adept. That's a person who's highly skilled at using his abilities. I also promise that we'll tell your mother as soon as she seems ready. Okay?"

"Okay, Mr. Powers," said Harry.

"You can stop calling me that. My name is Chance."

"Sure, Chance." That felt funny, for some reason. Mr. Powers didn't exactly fit, but neither did Chance. Harry wished he could call the man Daddy, but he didn't think either grown-up would approve. A man was either your father or he wasn't, and wishing wouldn't make it so.

A minute later, his mother came out carrying two suitcases. It was hard not to giggle when she saw the car and her mouth dropped open. "How on earth—?"

"We had a bit of luck," Chance said.

"How much did this luck cost?"

"Nothing."

She regarded him skeptically. "A tow truck just happened by and the driver volunteered to inflate my tires out of the goodness of his heart?"

"Trust me," said Chance, "it was an act of pure good-will."

Harry hoped she wasn't going to argue, and to his delight, she didn't. "Well, thank you," she said, opening the trunk. "But you're being more than generous, giving us a place to live in addition to a salary. I won't take advantage of you."

"I'm getting far more than my money's worth." Chance lifted her suitcases into the car. "Having an assistant at my beck and call will be a tremendous help."

Harry hoped the man would offer a ride in his sports car, and maybe he would have, but there was a tightness about Mom's mouth that warned she wasn't in the mood for any more favors. And maybe she wouldn't consider letting her son go for a high-speed whirl much of a favor, at that.

It didn't matter, Harry decided as he went back upstairs with his mom and Chance to collect the rest of their possessions. They were going to live with a real magician, and Harry was going to learn how to be one, too.

THERE WAS A CANYON intersection on the way to Chance's house that Tara could have sworn she'd seen before. The Art Deco mailbox in front of one house and the unusual angle at which the roads came together rang a bell in her memory, too.

But in Los Angeles, almost any site might have been used for a shoot. She supposed she could have seen this very intersection on television or in a film.

The blue sports car led the way, which was a good thing, because Tara doubted she could have followed Chance's written directions. The roads were so twisty, she hoped she wasn't going to get lost every time she tried to go back to his house.

As they drove, she realized this was the area in which she and Denise had taken such a disastrous wrong turn on that long ago Halloween. They'd figured later that, since they'd double-checked the street number, they must have been on the wrong road altogether. She could easily see how it must have happened.

Not for the first time, Tara wondered if she might be able to locate the castle again. But even if she found it, what would she do? Walk right up and introduce a total stranger to his son?

He probably moved out long ago. Or he's married. In any event, contacting the man would mean opening a Pandora's box.

Maybe someday she would try to find him, but she planned to wait until Harry was in his teens. By that age, she doubted any judge would wrench the boy away from home even if the father did hire a fancy lawyer.

Tara hadn't wanted to lie to Harry, so she'd told him simply that some men weren't ready to be fathers. He had asked if some women weren't ready to be mothers, a question that gave her pause until she remembered a friend who was adopted, and explained that yes, some moms weren't ready, either.

A few blocks later, the sports car turned into a driveway that ran through a wooded lot. Eucalyptus and pine trees filtered the sunlight and gave the air a shimmering clarity, as if they were entering the realm of fairy tales.

They emerged into a small glade with a house set at the far end. The scent of pine filled the car, and Harry bounced in his seat.

"It's like being in the mountains!" he crowed as she parked. "Are we really going to live here? Can I have a tree house?"

"That's up to Mr. Powers," Tara said.

"He told me to call him Chance."

"Well, don't get too familiar," she warned, without much hope of success. "He's my boss."

As soon as she killed the engine, Harry flung himself out. Dashing through pine needles, he ran around the clearing as if exorcising the demons of city living.

Chance emerged from a three-car garage, which also sheltered a black Lexus and a faded station wagon that probably belonged to the housekeeper. "What a bundle of energy."

"He wears me out," Tara admitted. "Is all this land yours?"

"Yes. It's a little over an acre." From her trunk, he lifted the heaviest cases. She took two string-tied boxes and decided to leave the rest for later.

The lot was huge for this area, Tara thought, grateful that her son would have a chance to enjoy the open space. She hoped this job worked out.

At the front door, Chance addressed the house. "Today's password is Fennel."

"You've got yesterday's password," scoffed a nasal voice. "Again."

"Garlic," he said.

"Oh, all right." The bolt unworked itself. "Did you get a dog?"

"A dog?" Chance said as he picked up the suitcases.

"My motion sensors tell me someone is dashing around the place. It's not my fault I don't have eyes. And there's a guest with you. Is she going to be dining in? Rajeev forgot to defrost anything."

"We'll send out for pizza." Chance sighed. "House, this is Tara Blayne and that 'dog' is her son, Harry. They're going to be living here."

"Well, don't forget to tell them the password every day," grumped the voice.

To Tara, Chance said, "He's kind of snappish. I think he's frustrated because he and my car broke up."

"Excuse me!" growled the house with sarcastic emphasis. "Are you going to stand there all day, or what?"

"Maybe he's annoyed because he doesn't have a name," Tara teased. "House, would you like for us to think of one?"

"I like your name," said the house. "Tara. Wasn't that the mansion in *Gone With the Wind?*"

"I guess I *was* named after a house, wasn't I?" she said as they walked inside, with Harry scampering behind. "I never thought about it."

"You can't both be Tara," said Chance. "We'll have to give this some thought."

"How about Manderley?" said the house, citing the stately home from *Rebecca.*

"It burned down," Tara advised.

Inside, Chance punched some buttons on a pad. She wasn't sure whether he was resetting the alarm or turning off the computer voice, but it didn't propose any more names.

The living room might have been decorated by an Eastern potentate, with furnishings from southern and central Asia. Instinctively, Harry slowed his pace and, to Tara's relief, refrained from running his hands over the gleaming mahoganies and teaks.

As she identified the Cuban rhythms of a rumba issuing from within the house, she felt a moment's confusion. Why was she so certain they were about to enter a courtyard?

A few more steps and they stood in the arching entrance to a flagstone-paved space surrounded by the curving wings of the house. Directly ahead rose a second-story tower.

Recognition hit Tara like a stinging dust cloud, smashing full into her face. She could hardly breathe, her eyes burned and her throat ached.

She knew this place as if from a dream, but a dream that had recurred night after night. It was the kind of distant, emotion-filled memory that she associated with her parents' old home near Louisville, as if a vital part of her life had passed here.

She could have sworn she had ascended that staircase to the balcony. And another time, that she had watched a dark figure in a cloak descend it with imperious grace. But she also recalled the courtyard filled with people, gaily costumed and celebrating by lantern light.

There were so many fragmented images, jumbled together and overlaid with a heavy sense of nostalgia, that Tara wondered if she could have lived here in a previous life. Not that she believed in reincarnation, but what other explanation could there be?

"Do you ever let people shoot movies here?" she asked Chance. "I think I've seen this house before."

"No, but the previous owner may have," he said. "I bought it about nine years ago."

He was watching her closely, and Tara realized her behavior must look peculiar. Shaking off her disorientation, she tried to focus on the Latin rhythms issuing from a boom box.

The tantalizing beat of maracas resounded through the open space. To one side, a man and woman in Spanish-style costumes were executing the stylized movements of the dance with seductive grace. If she hadn't been so preoccupied with her sense of déjà vu, Tara would have noticed them at once.

Both were dark-skinned and had the handsome features she associated with people from India. But this dance was definitely Cuban.

The couple slid across the stones with sinuous precision, knees bent, legs almost liquid, but with scarcely any movement above the waist. They took small, flat steps, alternating quick and slow movements as the man whirled his partner.

There was something formal about their approach, not like two lovers sharing a dance. The pair kept their heads high, smiles plastered across their faces and their gazes sweeping their surroundings as if acknowledging an audience.

As the music stopped, the two stamped their feet and struck a pose. Harry began to applaud, and Tara and Chance joined in.

"Ah! So you are returned!" The man bent to switch off the boom box.

"Welcome to our household!" The woman came forward with hands outstretched, and Tara clasped them gladly. "You are Mrs. Blayne? I am Vareena Goreng and this is my brother Rajeev."

"Are you guys magicians, too?" blurted Harry.

"Magicians?" Tara felt that whirling confusion again. *Magician.* How had her son known to associate that word with this place? If only she could remember the name of the film, she would feel a lot less uneasy.

"No, no." The man hurried over. "I am the house-keeper and this is my sister."

"I love children," said Vareena. "But I am not ready to have any."

"Not until we win many trophies," explained her brother. "And she finds a husband."

At least one thing clicked into place for Tara. "You were practicing ballroom dancing for a competition!"

"We are new to the field," said Rajeev. "But rising rapidly! Oh, dear. I have forgotten to defrost anything for dinner. But the house has told you this already, eh?"

"We're ordering pizza!" Harry sang out with glee. Fast food, a staple in most households, was a rare treat for the Blaynes. Tara's budget hadn't often been able to cover anything fancier than the kind of pizza she made at home with tortillas.

"Please allow me to carry these." Rajeev scooped up the suitcases and Vareena insisted on taking the boxes from Tara.

They led the way into one wing, peppering Harry with questions and explaining everything from how often they fed the tropical fish in a huge indoor tank to how the courtyard was engineered so that rainwater ran into a drain and not into the house.

Chance brought up the rear. When Tara glanced at him, he was watching her intently.

But she didn't feel uncomfortable anymore. It was impossible not to relax with the exuberant Gorengs.

She'd never had to share her son before, Tara thought with a pang. He'd always been exclusively hers to love and comfort, with no other family members involved.

But she didn't mind sharing him, not if it made her son happy. Besides, he would still belong to her. These were only borrowed quarters, and someday these people would fade into memory, like everything else in Tara's past.

Chapter Four

Having a family around, even one he couldn't officially acknowledge, was throwing Chance's life into turmoil.

No more eating leftovers in front of the television. Friday night's pizza was followed on Saturday by an elaborate meal, cooked by Rajeev with help from his sister and featuring three kinds of rice, eggplant in peanut sauce, roasted vegetables and, for Harry, vegetarian hot dogs.

Late that night, when Chance wandered into the kitchen in search of orange juice, he found Tara sitting at the table reading a novel. Draped across a chair, long shapely legs showing through a slit in her sleep shirt, she was mussing her hair with one hand, feeding herself bits of leftover vegetables with the other and holding her book open with one elbow.

The small, modern chandelier bathed her in a soft glow. Standing in the doorway, viewing her from the side, Chance found himself longing to stroke her hair into place and touch the velvety curve of her cheek.

He knew that he could enter her mind again. He had felt the vibrations between them from the moment she walked into his office.

More than anyone he had ever met, Tara was susceptible to his wizardry. It would take only a moment for their eyes to meet and her breathing to quicken. Then Chance could lift her in his arms and carry her into his room.

They could experience again that amazing sense of oneness. He would fuse with her thoughts, and she with his. They would become a single being, complete and harmonious and capable of incredible pleasure.

But matters would never be that simple. They hadn't been simple the last time. Just look at the surprise their actions had produced.

A wave of guilt, a most unfamiliar sentiment, ran through Chance. He had gained an incredible son, and so had Tara, but it was she who'd borne the burden of altering her life, sacrificing her independence, facing the hardships of raising a child alone.

He hadn't intended to manipulate her that night. He'd been young, brash, self-absorbed. But he knew better now.

He had no right to play games with Tara Blayne's heart. It was not up to him to judge whether the joy they could share would be worth any pain that might follow.

If they were to have a future, she would have to come to Chance of her own accord, without magic. Living with her, seeing her vulnerable and unaware like this, meant that he must exercise great restraint. To do otherwise would be to betray her trust, and to prove himself unworthy of his son.

Quietly he withdrew, leaving Tara alone with her book. Chance made a mental note to stock her suite with a refrigerator and microwave so she wouldn't need to venture into this wing again at night. His will might be forged of steel, but even steel could melt at high temperatures.

On Sunday afternoon, while Harry devoted himself to playing video games, Chance escaped into his office in the rear wing of the house. It ran the width of the structure, with a large window overlooking a rear slope filled with wildflowers and succulents. Farther off, he could see the tile roof of his neighbor's house.

Logging onto the Internet, Chance downloaded stock market data and began running a program he had customized. Absorbed in his work, he scarcely noticed when Tara entered.

She waited until he came up for air, then asked, "Do you have time to show me what you're doing?"

"It's Sunday," he said automatically. "You're off duty."

"I thought the point of my living here was so I could work odd hours."

Swiveling in his chair, Chance tried to suppress his reaction to her slim shape in a cotton sweater and figure-hugging jeans. He was achingly aware of the small, round breasts that had once molded themselves to his mouth, and the natural feminine scent of flowers and desire.

Seven years hadn't dimmed his memory of her. Sometimes he wished that his brain, like Tara's, had shifted the experience into the realm of dreams. Only years of training had given Chance full access to parts of his consciousness that most people kept shielded.

Right now, a masculine ache reminded him that such knowledge was not always a good thing. It took considerable effort to continue the conversation on an ordinary plane. "I don't want to take advantage of you."

"You aren't." Pulling up a chair, Tara sat beside him. "But if I'm intruding, feel free to throw me out."

Chance didn't want to do that, even though it would probably help his concentration. "This is a program that analyzes ups and downs in the stock market and compares them with the performance of our timing service.''

"Timing service?''

"It monitors our mutual funds.'' He explained that he advised his clients to put part of their capital in mutuals, which invested in a variety of stocks, thus spreading the risk. Traditionally, mutual funds grew much faster than inflation and, over a period of years, provided a healthy return.

However, they still took a hit when the market suffered a dip. The function of a timing service was to analyze conditions, predict when the market was likely to drop and move the clients' money from the mutual funds into a money market account, then buy back into the funds later to take advantage when prices rose again.

"Kind of like what I would do if I paid close attention to the stock market and did a lot of buying and selling at the right time?'' Tara said.

"More or less.'' Explaining the complicated business helped keep Chance's body from hardening every time she leaned over him to look at the computer. "Of course, nobody's right all the time. The stock market can be unpredictable, even when the timer's system is basically valid. Just because they guess wrong once in a while, that doesn't mean I want to switch to a new timing service.''

She studied him with respect. "But you want to make sure they aren't wrong too often, for your clients' sakes.''

"Just as they keep on top of the stock market, I keep on top of the timing service,'' Chance agreed. "Now, here's how the program works....''

Tara was a quick study, as fast as any employee he'd had, particularly considering she'd never worked with stocks before. Before Chance realized it, twilight had fallen and Rajeev was calling them to dinner.

He hoped that her mental agility indicated that she would soon be able to grasp the concept that magical powers existed. Maybe, in a purely objective context, she would have been able to accept it now.

But the subject was tied up with his paternity and with Harry's future. It was too much to expect her to take more than one small step at a time.

Chance hoped he could determine what those steps ought to be and guide her smoothly. These days, he had to be an expert on timing in his personal life too, except that, unlike in business, he had no previous experience to draw on.

TARA WAS GLAD she'd worked on Sunday, because she had to take a half day off on Monday to enroll Harry in his new school.

The building had fresher paint and a newer playground than his old one, and the children looked better scrubbed. A couple of kids, she noticed, wore expensive outfits, and she hoped they weren't snobbish about clothing.

Harry's new teacher seemed cheerfully capable, and the class wasn't far ahead of where his old class had been. With only a couple of months left in the school year, she didn't want her son to get frustrated.

Driving back to Chance's house, she followed his hand-drawn map with care. Tara could almost have sworn the streets shifted a little and that some of the landmarks had changed since this morning.

With relief, she turned into the driveway and parked to one side. Chase had mentioned something yesterday about installing a carport for her, but she couldn't imagine that he would go to such lengths for an employee.

As she got out, Tara allowed herself a moment to breathe the fragrant air and enjoy the quiet. Since leaving Kentucky, she'd missed the sounds and scents of nature.

There was something special about this glade. The light had a sepia tone, as if it came from long ago. She could imagine magical things happening here.

The only magic Tara believed in, she reminded herself, was the kind that came from within the human heart. In a searing flash, as if her thoughts had been illuminated by lightning from a clear sky, she saw that Chance Powers might indeed be that kind of magician. He tempted her more than any man she had ever met.

Even when dealing with mundane matters, she never lost her awareness of his physical presence. His resonant voice reached within her like a challenge, or an invitation. Sometimes she felt as if she could reach inside him, too.

Tara could picture him clearly: the dark hair and gray eyes, the strong-boned face and provocative smile, the body taut with restrained power. In only a few days, he had become a dominant part of her mental landscape.

But she must resist him. If not, she risked losing her job and this wonderful place to live.

AT LUNCH, most of the kids bought the cafeteria food. There was a choice between a hamburger and a burrito. This school had a special lunchroom, instead of using the auditorium like his old school, and there was a salad bar, plus a yogurt machine.

Harry had let Rajeev pack an eggplant sandwich, which tasted good, but the other kids were giving him pained expressions. They had fancy clothes with names written across the front that Harry had seen on television commercials. And they wore the kind of sneakers that famous basketball players endorsed. It was like going to a whole school full of John Abernathys.

One other boy was sitting by himself at the end of the table. He was thin with short hair and thick glasses. Like the others, he wore big-name clothes and had bought his lunch, but nobody was talking to him.

"Hi," said Harry. "What's your name?"

"Al."

"I never met a kid named Al before."

"It's short for Alcindor but the other kids make fun of that."

"They shouldn't act mean."

The boy smiled. "What's your name?"

"Harry. Like Houdini."

"Who's Houdini? I mean—Who Dini?"

They both laughed.

"He's a guy who used to work magic tricks, just like—" Harry remembered his promise to Chance about keeping a secret. "Like at the circus."

"Wanna play tetherball?"

Harry didn't like knocking a ball around a pole, but who cared what they did, as long as he had a friend? "Sure."

They ran out of the lunchroom together, ignoring the looks from a couple of their classmates. Harry hoped there weren't any bullies who would pester him and Al.

That might make it hard to keep his word. He didn't want to let Chance down.

BY THURSDAY, Tara had begun to feel comfortable with Chance's computer programs and to learn how he worked with his clients. Some of them were famous and most were rich, but he treated the modest investors with the same care.

That afternoon, she rode to the office with him and began getting acquainted with his staff. To her relief, the others expressed delight in having someone to share the workload.

"Chance is a perfectionist," explained his executive secretary. "He works twice as hard as anyone else, and we feel like we're letting him down when we don't stay late. Having you here takes a burden off us."

"I'm glad to hear it." Tara gazed around the expansive office with its fresh-cut flowers on the desks. "It's worked out well for me, too."

She and Chance stayed after the other staff left. Rajeev and Vareena had arranged to pick up Harry and take him to their dance class, then out for fast food. Her son had been looking forward to the outing, including Rajeev's offer to tell him a bedtime story from Indian folklore.

"It's almost too good to be true," Denise said with a sigh when Tara called her during a coffee break. In the whirl of moving into a new home, she hadn't phoned her friend all week.

"Don't say that. It might be bad luck."

"I thought you didn't believe in luck," her friend teased.

"I don't. But I don't want to tempt fate in case I'm wrong."

After hearing the latest gossip from the salon and promising to call again soon, Tara went back to finish familiarizing herself with the computer files. Chance sent out for submarine sandwiches, and they ate dinner at their desks.

Being part of such a high-speed business made the adrenaline sing through her bloodstream. In a way, Chance was part of the excitement, she admitted silently. He certainly affected her. Whenever she came near, she felt as if she'd been magnetized and he were a rod of iron. Tara could almost feel the hairs on her arms standing on end.

She supposed it would have been safer to work for an unattractive man, or one who was married. Yet the current of electricity between them added a note of danger that kept her both alert and intrigued.

It was late by the time they knocked off, but Tara didn't feel tired. How could she when her body was buzzing and sparks kept lighting up her brain?

They rode down in the elevator and emerged into a balmy spring night. A gardener must have spent the afternoon working on the planters, because the leggy begonias had been replaced by pansies and snapdragons. The bright colors stood out even in the light of a street lamp.

Chance reached over and plucked a dozen of the tall blooms. Pulling out a handkerchief, he soaked it in water from a nearby sprinkler and wrapped it around the lower stems.

The man had flowers on every desk in the office. What on earth was he doing picking blooms out of the planters?

Distracted, Chance didn't notice her reaction at first, and then he glanced with amusement at the bouquet in his hand. "I suppose that must have looked odd."

"I don't know," she admitted. "Maybe you do it all the time."

"No, I—" For the first time since she'd known him, he appeared at a loss for words. "It was just, as we were coming down the elevator, I got the feeling—I mean—"

"You don't have to apologize." As they entered the parking structure, Tara waited for the car to unlock itself.

"I haven't seen my great-aunt Cynda in a long time." Both front doors popped open. "She only lives a mile from here and it occurred to me that we ought to stop and see her. That's why I picked the flowers. I hope you don't mind a side trip.''

Mentally, Tara checked off the time and the fact that her son would be in bed by now and probably asleep. "There's no hurry."

"You'll get a kick out of her." Chance slid behind the wheel and handed her the flowers. "Hold the heads down. They'll stay fresher that way."

A few blocks away lay major thoroughfares, but they took residential streets. The cottagelike homes and neat lawns might have belonged in a small town.

Chance's audacity in plucking the flowers amused Tara. There'd been a childlike spontaneity to his actions, and besides, he'd probably paid for the planting himself.

She hoped they wouldn't be imposing on his great-aunt. It was only eight o'clock, but perhaps the lady changed into her nightclothes early.

A few blocks later, they stopped in front of a three-story building made of beige brick. It might date to the 1930s or 1940s, Tara guessed.

They took the stairs to the top floor. "Aunt Cynda?" Chance knocked on the closest door. "It's me."

"What took you so long?" rapped a firm voice from inside. "I sent you a message an hour ago."

Tara wondered what his aunt meant about a message. Chance hadn't mentioned a phone call.

He opened the door and they stepped into a sprawling front room. She couldn't gauge its size because of the crush of furnishings.

A huge Chinese vase had been crammed next to a Regency love seat with no apparent thought to style or period. A Tiffany lamp cast its amber glow across a Danish modern shelf holding worn volumes with gold-embossed titles. It was hard to make out the color of the carpet for the clutter of tables and curio cabinets.

From a winged armchair arose a fragile-looking woman with black eyes. A crisp pantsuit indicated that the disorder in her decorating did not extend to her wardrobe.

"Well?" said the woman, and Chance strode forward, bending to bestow a dry kiss on her cheek.

"I should have come a long time ago, Aunt Cynda," he murmured. "You didn't have to summon me."

"I had good reason!" The peppery old lady gave her great-nephew a glimmer of a smile. "My, you do keep getting handsomer. Thank goodness you haven't lost the touch. I was afraid you didn't get my message."

"Message?" Tara asked.

"Mental telepathy!" Aunt Cynda turned her attention to the newcomer. "Don't tell me you're a nonbeliever!"

Tara didn't know how to respond, and Chance saved her the necessity by making introductions. As she thanked them for the flowers, his great-aunt continued to scrutinize Tara. Finally she said, "The girl doesn't know, does she?"

"Know what?" Tara asked.

"Aunt Cynda." A warning note darkened Chance's voice.

"Ah, well." After putting the snapdragons in a vase, the lady gestured them into two chairs that formed a semicircle with her own. In the center, on a small round table, sat a crystal ball. "I have a couple of items to discuss with you. Have you seen your father recently?"

"I dropped by at Christmas," Chance said. "The house was full of guests, so we didn't talk much."

"Well, he's up to something." Cynda turned to Tara.

''My nephew was always the sly one. Now he's got Lois working for him.''

''I'm sorry,'' she said, ''but I don't know who these people are.''

''My father is Raymond Powers, owner of Screen Magic Technologies,'' Chance explained. ''Lois is Aunt Cynda's granddaughter. She's twenty-two, just graduated last year from the University of Southern California.''

His great-aunt went on, expressing her mistrust of her nephew and her dislike of having Lois work for him. ''The girl doesn't know what ethics are. She's not a bad child, but she's confused. Like a lot of people, she wants to be a big success without reckoning the costs.''

With scarcely a pause to breathe, the woman continued. ''Now her mother, Freya, she's mixed-up and she knows it. Everybody knows it. I should never have named her after the Norse goddess of love. She's been married four times and can't even remember which husband was Lois's father. We'd have to check the dates on the marriage licenses, if she still has them.''

''So you'd like me to find out what Lois is doing?'' Chance asked.

''You don't have to do any snooping,'' the woman muttered. ''Just get in touch with her and keep your eyes open. And other faculties, the ones we're not supposed to discuss.'' She gave Tara a meaningful look. ''You don't believe in the hidden powers of the mind, do you, child? Well, you should. Everyone has such powers to a degree. You must read this.''

From a side table, Aunt Cynda lifted a leather-bound volume that was open partway. To her surprise, Tara saw that the pages had been written by hand, in black ink.

''I am, informally, the family historian,'' explained their hostess, shutting the book. ''Recently I began getting strange images in my ball." She indicated the crystal ball, and Tara wondered if this might be some kind of monitor hooked up to the Internet.

"Regarding my father and Lois?" Chance asked.

"No, no!" His great-aunt waved impatiently. "About you, of course. You and this young lady, in fact."

"Me?"

"Do you see any other young ladies present?" rasped the elderly woman. "Really, Chance, you should tell her about your family." To Tara, she said, "I don't suppose you know anything about past lives?"

"Reincarnation?" From the moment she'd entered the room, Tara had felt off center, as if the floor weren't solid, but she'd attributed that to the dim light and claustrophobic decor. Now her chair seemed to be sinking into a marsh, and yet it hadn't moved.

"The two of you should not have met this time around," Aunt Cynda went on. "Really, you've stirred up the most awful mess. You had a past life together, you see. I found it in this book. I could see your images laid over the page, both of you."

"My image?" Tara wished she could make sense of the woman's ramblings. "But you didn't know what I looked like until a moment ago."

"Not the details, perhaps, especially not that mop of hair—you should change the style, it's unbecoming—but your essence, indeed I did." Aunt Cynda thrust the book into Chance's hands. "Read the part I marked. Take it home with you."

Tara wasn't sure what to make of Chance's great-aunt. Topics poured out of the woman in a bewildering torrent, past lives and crystal balls all jumbled together. The woman's mind was like her apartment.

Accepting the book, Chance thanked his great-aunt. "I promise to give it my closest attention."

"Yes, well, I don't know how you're going to straighten this mess out!" Cynda said. "It all started when your father tried to stack the deck. Marrying his cousin just to concentrate the powers! Do read this and tell me what you think. And if you see Lois, tell me what you think of her, too. It's all this self-esteem nonsense they teach children in school. She thinks she's wonderful, but what's she wonderful at, tell me that!"

"I'll keep in touch," Chance said. "Let me know if there's anything you need."

"Nothing, nothing." The woman turned her attention back to Tara. "Sorry if I've made a bad impression. Freya tells me I have a motor mouth, but at least I don't keep going through the revolving door in a Las Vegas wedding chapel. I wonder the woman doesn't pick men with the same first name so she won't have to worry which one she calls out in her sleep."

"Good night, dear." Chance brushed another kiss across her cheek.

"It's been a pleasure meeting you." Tara meant it, even though she hadn't followed half of what had been said.

They emerged into the clear night. Above, stars laced the heavens, and Tara felt a surge of gratitude when her queasiness evaporated.

She turned to Chance, and felt her chest squeeze. Overlying his familiar sculpted face, she saw the image of another man, dark and exotic and tender and alarmed, and painfully familiar.

Chapter Five

The dismay in Tara's expression alerted Chance that Aunt Cynda's comments must have disturbed her. As the car door opened automatically, he helped her into the seat. "Take a deep breath, then tell me what's wrong."

She blinked, her face close to his. "I thought I saw someone—like a double image—laid over you. I thought I knew him, but..." She shook her head.

Had she been remembering him as the Magician, or actually seen his image from a shared past life? Chance believed that people were, in a way, like computers. Under certain circumstances, they could plug into a universal consciousness, a sort of metaphysical Internet that could show them the past or future.

Tara wasn't ready to go this far this fast. She didn't even believe her son could zap a spoon in midair.

"It might have been the incense that made you dizzy," he said. "Did you notice it?"

Tara pressed her lips together before speaking. "No, I didn't."

Neither had Chance, but he needed an excuse that would calm her. "It can be disorienting."

"I'm sure I'll be fine after a night's sleep." Sinking into her seat, she stared out the windshield as if fascinated by the stars. They *were* brighter than usual tonight, Chance mused as he went around and started the engine.

He drove slowly, taking side roads to avoid the blare of lights and noise on the thoroughfares. Tara needed peace to restore her equilibrium.

"Why are we poking along?" complained the car in its edgy soprano. "There's no report of a traffic jam. There's no construction zones on my map."

He flipped a switch and the voice stopped. Once again, Chance wondered what masochistic impulse had made him create a computer personality that nagged. It must have seemed funny at the time.

At least the diversion served to rouse Tara. "I've been thinking about your aunt," she said. "How wonderful to have a family historian. How far back do your records go?"

"Orally, for close to a thousand years, but they've only been written down for about a century." Chance turned onto a major cross street. There didn't seem to be any further point in dawdling, now that Tara had regained her composure. "Since we came to this country."

"From where?"

"Eastern Europe," he said. "Possibly Romania. Bringing a full load of family legends, most of which I suspect are wildly exaggerated."

She straightened in her seat. "Family legends? That sounds exciting. I hardly know anything about my ancestors."

"Do you know where they came from?"

"Ireland and Scotland, on my father's side," Tara said. "My mother died when I was twelve, but she did mention being part French. And there was some Native American but I don't even know what tribe."

Streetlights and illuminated signs cast fleeting shadows

across her face. The contributions of many ancient peoples showed in her pronounced cheekbones and olive eyes.

Had he met her before, in another body and another time? Did he feel such a strong link to her because of a previous relationship, or was that wishful thinking?

Whatever the cause, he had felt from the moment they met that their souls were intertwined. In a subliminal way, he had been part of Tara's life, and she of his, since birth.

Sneaking sidelong glances as he drove, he tried to puzzle out what it was about the lady that drew him so strongly. Certainly she was attractive, but he'd met other women more conventionally beautiful. There was something else, a primal attraction that defied explanation.

Maybe Aunt Cynda was right and they'd shared a past life together. Or was he trying to elevate a normal emotional response into something supernatural?

When they arrived home, the house lay quiet. Floodlights bathed the yard as soon as they drove in.

"Rajeev and Vareena and the boy are home," the house advised when Chance logged in today's password. "What do you think of Windsor Castle?"

"As a name for you? Too fancy."

"I suppose Mount Vernon is out, too," grumbled the house.

"Something warmer," Tara suggested. "More welcoming."

"Pooh Corner?" said the house. "Oh, spare me."

They entered the living room. Normally, Chance would have headed for his bedroom, which lay to the right, and allowed Tara to turn left, toward hers.

Tonight, however, he felt an overwhelming urge to protect her. Although Rajeev and Vareena's quarters lay along the way to Tara's, he felt an old-fashioned need to escort her.

She didn't object when he set his aunt's book on a coffee table and walked with her into the hall. Only a faint electrical whir underlay the stillness of the house.

At the end of the hall, they entered Tara's den. It was the front room of a second master suite, a twin to Chance's, that had been mostly unused until her arrival.

A light flicked on automatically, casting a golden circle across the couch. Scattered on the cushions were a couple of video-game magazines, obviously belonging to Harry.

Inside the smaller of the two bedrooms, a tiny figure curled beneath a quilt on the bed. Harry had fallen asleep while reading a book about tornadoes, which his mother gently moved aside.

Through the window, moonlight played across the small figure, revealing his tousled hair and the thick lashes curved against his soft cheek. Tenderness rushed through Chance and he yearned to scoop the boy into his arms.

In the past few days, he had watched Harry segue through his moods, from boisterous to cranky, merry to exhausted, bold to apprehensive. Now he saw another side—the vulnerability of babyhood.

Chance's heart twisted as he pictured Tara, alone, determinedly meeting the boy's needs and standing guard over him all these years. He wished he could have been there. But at least he was here now.

Tara signaled, and they tiptoed out. She, too, looked sleepy and defenseless, and he felt a touch of guilt for keeping her out. It was after ten o'clock, not terribly late, but she had put in a long day.

Without thinking, he slipped one arm around her waist, and she leaned against him. The movement felt so natural

that they might have done the same thing many times
before.

Drawing her close, he brushed his lips across her hair.
An unbecoming mop, his aunt had called it, but he liked
the waiflike air it gave her.

Tara's slender, slightly angular body came to the perfect height to nestle against his. Her face met the curve
of his shoulder and her hip fit within the shelter of his
thigh.

Unbidden, his heart rate speeded up. He heard her
breath come more quickly, too.

Was she as keenly aware of him as he was of her? He
could feel the points of her breasts harden, and the heat
surge through her veins. In a moment her lips would part
and her head tilt back—yes, she was doing it now—and
then his mouth came down on hers.

His tongue probed, at first tentatively, then with more
command. They melted into each other, the air silvering
around them. As he felt himself tightening with desire,
Chance experienced her awakening hunger, as well.

It was as if their minds as well as their bodies had
become entangled. They were entering each other the
way they had on that night long ago.

Chance needed to know more about what lay between
them before he risked making love to Tara again. Merging with her at this point might even cause her harm, and
he couldn't bear that.

Reluctantly he pulled back. She blinked up at him,
confused.

"I'm sorry," he murmured. "I was taking advantage
of your exhaustion."

She didn't protest as he steered her toward the larger
bedroom, then let her go in alone. She turned to watch
him with hooded eyes, and Chance experienced a longing

so intense, he could barely restrain himself from sweeping her onto the bed.

Instead, he spun and marched out of the suite.

TARA STOOD in the bedroom, her heart thundering. What had just happened between her and Chance?

Embarrassment heated her cheeks. She couldn't even remember which of them had initiated the embrace, but certainly she should have called a halt.

They were employer and employee, with the awkward additional circumstance that they lived in the same house. Both of them should know better than to risk any physical involvement.

Blood was still racing through her arteries, and she could feel the tautness in her breasts. She wanted him so much that, despite her better judgment, she half wished he had acted on his instinct to sweep her onto the bed.

Yet how did she know what his instincts were? Tara blinked, forcing herself to examine her thoughts. Oddly, she had the conviction that she had entered his mind while they were embracing.

She had felt his masculine need and seen her feminine warmth through his eyes. Could this be some lingering effect of Aunt Cynda's incense? What was in that stuff, anyway?

The most disturbing part was that Tara could have sworn she'd had this experience before. Once, she had entered a man's mind and seen herself from his point of view. But when could that have been?

For one flicker of an instant, she thought she had it. A magician—a mask—a cape. Then the image vanished into that part of the brain reserved for dreams.

She was just tired. That had to be the explanation. She

wasn't even sure whether she and Chance had embraced just now or whether she had imagined it.

THE BOOK CAUGHT Chance's eye as he passed through the living room on the way to his suite. He collected it with the intention of reading it tomorrow.

But when he reached his rooms, he couldn't find a place to put it. It might slide off the small table and suffer damage; on the couch, he might sit on it by accident, and the shelves were already crammed with too many books and CDs.

Without making a conscious decision, he walked into the courtyard. Once he'd gone that far, it made sense to climb the staircase to the tower.

The round room smelled stale from disuse. He ordered the computer to unlock a window, and open it to the night.

Cool air blew in, flavored with springtime. Unlike the rest of the house, this chamber didn't automatically light itself when he entered, and the darkness lay upon him like a balm.

He had intended to store the volume in a hidden bookcase, but sleep seemed far away. As long as he was here, Chance might as well read the passage his aunt had marked.

"Desk!" he said. Partitions slid aside in the wall and a desk, chair and reading lamp rotated out.

Settling onto the carved chair, he told the computer to turn on the lamp, laid the heavy volume on the desk and opened it to the place marked by a worn velvet ribbon attached to the binding.

The handwritten words swam before Chance's eyes, and he wondered if it were too late at night for reading. He closed his eyelids to rest them, and immediately a picture of Tara formed. Her face was soft, near sleep, yet he could feel desire pulsating beneath the surface.

She had begun to yield to him tonight exactly the way she had seven years ago, almost as if hypnotized. Was he unintentionally exerting power over her?

He must find out why they were so susceptible to each other, and what sort of things Cynda believed they were stirring up. Leaning forward, he forced the handwriting into focus.

"...Rudolf fathered Otemar and Magda, who was the mother of Luther, who was wed with Ilona of Moldavia. Ilona bore Luther four dead infants and one who lived but whose name is lost, only that he was the father of Valdemar and grandfather of Halden, the bastard, possessor of the far vision...."

Chance decided to check the previous page to find out when and precisely where these ancestors had lived. When he tried, however, he found it impossible because the book gave such dates as "in the fourth year of the reign of Prince Stefan" and such locations as "near the battleground of Seldonia."

With a sigh, he returned to the marked pages to find out more about Halden the illegitimate, who was born with the gift of seeing the future. But it was not, he soon saw, the story of Halden himself but of his parents that filled these pages.

Extracting the facts from the archaic language, Chance learned that Valdemar had fallen in love with a lady named Ardath, a fair woman who came from far away. But she was married to a cruel man, the Count of Fredaria, who had kidnapped her from her homeland.

While the count was away at war, Ardath and Valdemar ran off and hid themselves in a forest. After she bore a son, they determined to kill the count upon his return so they could marry.

"They did mingle their spirits, and went together to the count's castle to sicken him so that he would die." That was vague enough that it could mean almost anything, Chance grumped to himself. Mingle their spirits how? Sicken him with what? And what had they done, walked up to the front door and announced themselves?

"The count fell to the floor of his dining chamber, weakened but not killed, and a candle was overturned. A flame sprang up, consuming the lovers. The count ordered their son slain, but he was taken to a cottage by his kin and raised in secret."

Through the spare words, Chance felt the pain and terror of that moment. Before he could grasp what was happening, he lost all awareness of the tower, as if he had suddenly become someone else, or himself in another existence.

He stood in a long, dank room. Icy droplets seeped from the stone walls and foul-smelling mold crept along the woven hangings. Near the head of a great table, a candelabra cast elongated shadows across a coarse man with a ragged beard.

Reaching for his silver goblet, the count quaffed wine that glowed ruby red. He did not see Chance and Tara lingering in the shadows, for their minds were joined in suppressing his thoughts. He did not taste the tang of the poison as he sipped it.

Chance realized they had been controlling the count's mind, drawing strength from a love so forceful it linked his soul to Tara's. Driven by desperation, the two of them had formed a psychic link that gave them formidable power.

His scarred face contorting in pain, the count slumped

forward. His hand brushed a candelabra, knocking it onto the table. As the man slid to the floor, a piece of cloth flared.

The thud of his fall summoned a servant, who screamed for the guards. They reached the dining hall as the fire spread, and pulled their master to safety.

Retching up the poison as he was hauled away, the count recovered himself enough to see the figures in the shadow. "Death to the assassins!" he rasped. "Leave them in the flames!"

Thick smoke filled the air. Heat scorched Chance's face, but worst of all were Tara's cries. She was sobbing not for herself but for their little son, Halden, and what would become of him left orphaned and alone.

He tried to push her to safety, but guards thrust forward their long lances, forcing her back. Either way lay death. As the killing fumes choked him, Chance sank to his knees, gasping, refusing to believe the end had come, vowing to return and make things right...

With a groan, he tore himself back to the present. A cool breeze murmured through the tower window and eased the smarting of his skin.

He could still smell the acrid smoke and hear Tara's screams. The scene seemed more real than this house and this time.

Brushing back a hank of hair, he began to pace. Aunt Cynda's gifts were limited, but well-defined. She saw little of the future but much of the past, which was why she had assumed the role of family historian.

She had seen that Chance and Tara were Valdemar and Ardath in a previous lifetime, and she had been right to notify him. Their story echoed with unresolved longings, with anguish and with the need to put things right.

Pausing by the window, Chance stared down into the

courtyard. Small white Malibu lights pricked the darkness, outlining the curving spaces with fairy-tale fragility. As if the computer were amusing itself, the fountain sprang to life, flinging glittering droplets into the night in a soothing play of pink and blue lights, before falling silent again.

He had sensed since adolescence that it would be wrong to abuse his powers. His father, of course, had disagreed, calling him selfish and shortsighted for refusing to take advantage of others. Sometimes Chance had wondered how he came by such a fierce determination to stick to his principles.

Now he saw the temptation and the danger more clearly than ever. Valdemar and Ardath, blinded by their love for each other and their hatred of the count, had joined their minds to attempt murder.

It had backfired. The count had survived, and their son was left alone.

Now they were living again, in new bodies. There was no evil count here. But now, as then, they had created a son together.

Perhaps it was the emotional echoes of the story, but Chance got a strong sense, as Cynda had also, that his reunion with Tara had revived an unresolved conflict. Anything left unfinished, in any lifetime, would seek to close the circle.

Would they be tempted to misuse their psychic link again? That would be playing with fire, figuratively if not literally.

Chance could not and would not remove Tara from his life. But what had happened between them that night seven years ago must never be allowed to happen again.

Chapter Six

It wasn't a formal softball game, but the kids were getting excited, including Harry. He jumped up and down after he hit the ball and ran two bases, sending one player home.

They were still behind, 3-2, but Sammi was on third base and he was on second. All the next batter needed to do was get to first base, and they'd at least tie the score before the recess bell sounded.

"Who's next?" yelled Sammi, shaking her dark-blond ponytail. As the best player in the first grade, she got to boss other people around.

"Me! Me! It's my turn!" Al loped forward, tried to snatch the bat from the ground and missed. He had to turn around and bend to pick it up.

Harry's heart sank. In the past few days, he'd enjoyed Al's friendship, and it was fun swapping secret codes for video games. But the boy couldn't hit a ball to save his life.

"Let somebody else play!" shouted Sammi, and the other kids chorused their agreement.

Behind his thick glasses, Al's face crumpled. "But I got skipped last time!" His voice quavered. "It's my turn. You're not being fair!"

Sammi made a quick check to be sure the playground monitor wasn't watching, then yelled, "We want to win, you wimp! Now get out of here!"

Harry wanted to win, too. But it wasn't fair to make Al miss two turns. Besides, he knew what his mom would say, that the point wasn't to win but for everyone to have a good time.

"Let him play!" he shouted. "Come on, Sammi. Fair's fair!"

Her mouth twisted as she glared at him, but then she shrugged. "If you say so."

The first time Al swung at an impossibly high ball and missed, Harry winced. The second time, when Al tried to hit a ball so far from the bat it was nearly to Mongolia, the other kids groaned.

The pitcher was grinning. Staring into her cocky freckled face, Harry listened to her thoughts. *I could fling anything at the little sucker, and he'd go for it.*

His hands got sweaty. It was the first time he'd heard anybody thinking. Was this more of the magic he and Chance had talked about?

Mostly he was sweating because this girl was going to strike Al out. Harry hadn't meant to let his team down.

Why did he have to pick between what was fair to his friend and what would make the others happy? And why did Al have to be such a lousy player?

Again, Harry caught the drift of the pitcher's thoughts. She was going to throw the next ball low. *It's cinchy! We win!*

It wouldn't take much to correct the girl's aim. Just a little concentrated attention on Harry's part, a slight tweak upward—why, he could make it smack right into Al's bat! Even a bunt would be enough to send Sammi to home plate.

The pitcher began rotating her arm, and then, after an impossibly long time, the ball launched itself forward. For Harry, everything slowed as he poured his energy into that small orb, easing it upward, getting it in line with the bat.

But he'd promised Chance not to use his powers where other people might see. He'd given his word!

With a wrench, Harry tore his thoughts from the ball. Still in slow motion, watching in horror, he saw the thing wobble in midair and drop downward, passing beneath the flailing bat.

From behind his glasses, Al stared in disbelief at the empty air. Everyone else was staring, too. The recess bell went off like an earthquake warning siren, so loud it made Harry jump.

The other team cheered. Sammi's face was a volcano about to explode. Other kids stalked by Al, not looking at him, and the boy began to cry.

In trying to help, Harry had made things worse. Nobody could have hit that weird ball, the way it had jerked in midair, and it was his fault.

Feeling miserable, he trudged over to put his arm around Al's shoulders, the way he'd seen athletes do on TV. No one spoke to them as they walked to class, and Al didn't stop crying until he'd used up all the tissues in his desk.

Harry stared at his New Math book, with its little blobby shapes that he was supposed to sort and count until his teeth hurt from sheer boredom. The blobs looked like baseballs, every one of them jeering at him.

He needed to have a serious talk with Chance.

SITTING BESIDE CHANCE at his desk, trying to ignore the inviting dance of late-afternoon sunlight through the trees outside, Tara watched her employer zap a message into the computer. Around them, the airy home office hummed with the energy emanating from its owner.

Every time she observed him at work, she became more impressed with Chance's abilities. He was knowledgeable and thorough, checking and rechecking his facts.

Right now, he was E-mailing a group of his more-risk-taking clients to recommend purchase of stock in a genetic engineering firm. Such companies, he'd explained earlier, had been hot when they first came on the market, then sagged as they failed to produce major breakthroughs.

Chance kept tabs on a variety of firms whose stock he considered undervalued. In this case, he'd been reading medical journals and summaries of seminars and conferences.

He believed one particular company was on the verge of winning FDA approval to test an exciting new treatment for diabetes. It would be illegal to manipulate stocks on the basis of inside information, so everything Chance had learned was available to the general public. But hardly anyone had the expertise and determination—and perhaps the instincts—to do the right research.

No wonder people called him a wizard. Tara smiled to herself. She lacked his talent but was learning quickly, and there were moments when she could almost read Chance's mind. They worked well together.

"Incoming message!" A few keystrokes, and the first of the client responses popped into view: "Go for it!"

"All right!" Tara cheered.

"Let's hope I'm right about this one," Chance cautioned, but he didn't appear worried as he began executing the buy order.

When he was finished, he leaned back in the chair and stretched, his polo shirt taut across his wide shoulders. Tara could feel his muscles beneath her hands as she held him last night....

Last night? Confused, she tried to make sense of the random thought. The only thing that had happened yesterday was that they'd returned home late from Cynda's apartment and Tara had fallen into bed, exhausted.

She must have dreamed about Chance. Some of her dreams were quite vivid. She even remembered how it had felt to hold him. He had been solid and powerful, and she could smell the muskiness that bespoke ·awakening passion.

Tara gave herself a mental slap. A person couldn't control her dreams, but she must not fantasize about her boss. For a lot of reasons, she needed to keep Chance at arm's length.

Certainly he'd been all business when he returned from his main office this morning after leaving Tara to sleep late. His plan had been to take the afternoon off, but then he'd skimmed some medical abstracts from a just-ended seminar and here he was, helping his clients earn money.

"Think you can keep tabs on the messages and place the orders?" he asked. Tara nodded eagerly, pleased when he let her handle the next one.

"You're a quick study," he said. "I'll put in a call to Cousin Lois. I did promise Aunt Cynda to make sure she's all right."

"Why wouldn't she be?"

"My dad has an old-fashioned sense of business ethics." Chance's mischievous grin turned his gray eyes to silver. "'Old-fashioned' as in pillaging and looting. We wouldn't want him corrupting my innocent young cousin."

The screen flashed an alert of another incoming message, and for the next few minutes Tara was too busy to do more than register the fact that her boss was on the phone. Then Chance signaled her and put his call on hold.

"Lois wants us to come for dinner tonight," he said. "You and me. What do you think?"

"Why on earth would she invite me?" Tara was surprised that such a young woman would even think about giving a dinner party, let alone welcome a stranger.

"Apparently Aunt Cynda told her about our supposed past lives," Chance said. "She thinks it's cute."

He'd sketched the bizarre story for Tara at lunch, about illicit lovers in some bygone century who'd tried to murder a count and had died in a blaze instead. It was true that she'd always had a particular fear of fire, but that wasn't unusual. "I'd love to meet Lois, but I'm afraid we'd be imposing."

"She insists," he said, and, receiving a nod, conveyed her acceptance to his cousin.

After hanging up, he checked Tara's work and was complimenting her when the door from the courtyard banged open and Harry barreled through. Behind him, Rajeev, who had picked the boy up at school, shrugged apologetically.

"Honey, Mr. Powers is working," Tara began, but Chase waved down the admonition.

"It's all right," he said. "He looks upset. What's the matter?"

"Oh, it's—at school—these kids were playing softball," the little boy blurted. "I tried to help my friend, but then I stopped, and it messed things up worse."

The words didn't make sense to Tara, but Chase seemed to understand. "I guess it's time we practiced."

"Practiced what?" Tara asked.

Two faces turned toward her, wearing identical startled expressions. Sometimes it amazed her how much the two resembled each other, especially their eyes, although Harry's hair was much lighter than Chance's.

"Technique," said her boss.

"You're teaching him to play softball?" she said in surprise.

"Not exactly." He shifted uncomfortably. "Although it relates to softball. I guess you might call it hand-eye coordination."

"Couldn't she watch us?" asked Harry.

Chance nodded thoughtfully. "Yes, of course she could. Tara?"

Another message was incoming on the computer, she noticed. Besides, although from time to time she helped Harry practice his pitching and catching, it wasn't an activity she relished. "You go ahead."

"Thanks, Mom." Her son gave a happy hop. "When I get really good, you can watch me."

"I'd love to," she said as the two of them hurried out.

Harry was trying to match Chance's powerful stride. He couldn't imitate the older man's grace, but the two had the same easy swing from the hips. It was uncanny.

CHANCE WONDERED if he'd made a mistake by insisting his son abstain from magic in public. The kid looked as if his heart were breaking because he and his friend had muffed one softball game.

But he couldn't let Harry run around manipulating objects with no idea of what the implications might be. In addition to the fact that it would attract too much attention, it could tempt the boy into cheating his way through life.

As they tossed a softball in the driveway, it became clear that the boy already knew how to guide an object. He could make it go straight up, bob sideways or hook downward and then fly up again.

"I guess it wouldn't be fair to do that, huh?" Harry said. "But that pitcher made me mad. She kept thinking about what a sucker Al was."

A chill ran up Chase's spine. He'd been in high school when the voices began. By then, he'd had enough sophistication to recognize how odd the phenomenon was and to worry, for a few scary weeks, that he might be suffering a mental breakdown.

Careful observation had shown that his "voices" accurately predicted other people's subsequent actions. It was a relief to realize he was reading other people's minds, not losing his.

For a while, he had mischievously tuned in to teachers and classmates. Soon, though, he realized he was invading their privacy. Besides, it would be too easy to abuse the knowledge he gained, especially about the girls who wanted to date him.

His error had been to ask his father for help. Chase had assumed Ray, too, could read thoughts, but he'd discovered not only that it wasn't true but that his father wanted him to snoop on a business rival.

Faced with pressure to harness his ability for personal gain, Chase did his best to stop reading minds. For a while, he persuaded his father that he'd been mistaken, but then came the night of the near-accident when Ray saw him manipulate the little girl out of the path of the truck.

That was the beginning of the conflict that finally drove him away from his father's business. By now, steeling his mind against other people's thoughts had become second nature, even—most of the time—where Tara was concerned.

It had shocked him at first, when her thoughts penetrated his mental barrier. Then he'd realized that she was reading his mind as well, although she had no other magical abilities.

Their psychic link from a previous lifetime, interrupted in its full flower, must have been reborn. The frightening part was that their son had inherited such precocious talents.

Harry needed guidance. And Chance was here to give it to him.

"The problem," he said, "isn't the ball. It's the way you got inside the pitcher's mind. It's not fair to do that, even though it was an accident."

He gestured to his son to sit beside him on a low stone wall, and Harry hurried over. Now came the tricky part.

Before the boy could erect a barrier around his mind, he had to exercise his power until he understood its nature. The easiest way would be to practice on strangers who would never know the difference.

Of course, that raised the possibility that Harry would become adept and then refuse to give it up. But it appeared that his mother had instilled a firm sense of values.

"Let's drive to the video store," Chance said. "I know a game we can play. But you only play it with me, and never to trick or hurt people, okay?"

"Sure." Harry grinned at him with complete trust. "This should be fun!"

"No, NO! You move your shoulders too much!" Rajeev paused the CD, then clicked it to repeat the song.

"The problem is you!" retorted his sister. "You are bouncing. The cha-cha is done on the flat of the foot!"

She glanced at Tara as if for support, but Tara shrugged apologetically. She had no idea how the cha-cha was supposed to be executed, but to her unpracticed eyes, the brother and sister were doing a remarkable job.

She'd heard them practicing as she finished her work in the office, and she'd come into the courtyard to watch. Twilight was falling now, and, in response, the computerized floodlights shifted gradually to full strength.

"I was stepping back!" Rajeev returned. "It is impossible to do that on the flat of the foot."

"You aren't supposed to step back! You are supposed to lead."

He turned off the boom box. "We have practiced enough for today. We are fighting."

"We are not fighting! I am right and you are wrong, but you are too stubborn to admit it!" His sister glared at him, then began to smile. "So. You were bouncing and I was moving my shoulders. We were both wrong."

"Yes, yes, that is true. Our school's competition is less than two months away," Rajeev explained to Tara. "I think we will not be ready."

"It's worth competing just to gain the experience, I should think," she pointed out.

"Yes! Exactly," said Vareena. "Well, we can practice a little more, since we have leftovers for dinner."

"There are no leftovers in the refrigerator," advised the computer from a hidden speaker. "Rajeev ate them for his afternoon snack."

"I will cook!" he said quickly, to forestall his sister's wrath. "Come, Vareena. One more run through!"

As she listened to the opening bars of the music, Tara wondered why Chance and Harry were taking so long at the video store. But she was glad the two of them had hit it off.

Still, she didn't want Harry to become too attached. Her job here might last a few months or a few years, but it was temporary. It would be terrible if he began thinking of Chance as his father, only to lose him.

In front of her, the brother and sister resumed the Latin dance. This time, they kept their movements more level, with less bobbing on both sides.

Oddly, she could see herself dancing in this courtyard, long ago. She was swaying in Chance's arms, their movements so light her feet scarcely touched the flagstones.

He sensed each shift of her body, reflecting her slightest inclination so closely that she felt as if their bodies were melting together. It was like last night, when they'd embraced—except they hadn't. It had been a dream. Both times, a dream.

She yawned, gulping in the cool air. This daydreaming wasn't like her. She felt like a schoolgirl, fantasizing about a boy on whom she had a crush.

Rajeev and Vareena had just finished dancing when Harry darted into the courtyard, with Chance following. Both of them wore bemused expressions.

"That was fun!" Harry declared.

"What did you rent?" Tara asked.

"Rent?" Her son blinked, puzzled.

Embarrassment flashed across Chance's face. "We were playing a game, trying to figure out which tapes other people would rent. We forgot to get one ourselves."

"We can play a board game tonight," Vareena suggested. "There is no need for videos."

"You're both so kind to baby-sit," Tara said. "I'm sorry to be gone two evenings in a row."

"It is fun for us!" said Rajeev.

"Maybe I shouldn't—"

"It's a bit late to back down," Chance said. "Lois would be very disappointed."

"Who's Lois?" Harry asked.

"Your cousin." His words hung in the air for a moment before he corrected himself. "I mean, my cousin."

"You're right. I can't cancel now," Tara conceded. "I'd better go change."

LOIS'S NEW ADDRESS turned out to be the penthouse unit in a swank building on Wilshire Boulevard. Chance took in the elegant lobby and paneled elevator with growing dismay.

"Wow," Tara said as they emerged on the top floor. "How does a recent college graduate afford a place like this?"

"That's a good question."

Ray paid his top employees well, but only if they made contributions that helped his business. That category included special-effects designers and innovators at computer graphics, not business graduates with the ink still wet on their diplomas.

His cousin had graduated near the top of her class, but she lacked experience. Chance had never heard that the girl had any particular psi talents, either.

If she weren't psychic, she must be willing to aid and abet whatever schemes his father was devising. With his attention occupied by Tara and Harry, Chance wasn't sure he had the energy or interest to rescue his cousin from her own character flaws.

But he had promised Aunt Cynda that he would help. Maybe a few well-chosen warnings were all it would take to bring Lois to her senses.

As he listened to the doorbell echo inside the spacious apartment, he wondered how corruptible his young cousin was. Her choice of an apartment showed a taste for luxury, which was not a good sign.

On the other hand, he recalled Lois from family get-togethers as a bright, articulate young woman, eager to learn and quick to question those around her. Surely she would soon realize that there was more to life than enriching oneself at the expense of others.

Perhaps he could find a place for her in his own company. Chance was considering opening a Northern California office, which would mean relocating some of his top staff and creating several positions locally. He couldn't pay an inexperienced staffer enough to afford a place like this, but there would be advancement opportunities.

Then the door swung open. Standing there, bright-faced and welcoming, was his cousin, her dark hair cut in a chic wedge and her designer suit made of ultrasoft silk.

Standing right behind her, his square-jawed face slashed by a calculated smile, waited Raymond Powers.

Chapter Seven

The tension between Chance and his father was evident from the moment the two locked gazes in the doorway, bracing themselves in a way that reminded Tara of two wolves sizing each other up.

She knew from comments Chance had made over the past few days that the two had parted company over some disagreement on ethics. But that didn't explain why Raymond had chosen to attend this dinner.

Of the four of them, only Lois seemed at ease. In fact, as she guided them into the sunken living room where a uniformed maid was serving cocktails, she seemed to delight in playing hostess.

It didn't take a genius to see that tonight's invitation hadn't been a spontaneous expression of hospitality. Lois was helping her boss play some game, and relishing the opportunity.

As they made introductions and exchanged pleasantries, Tara tried to sort out her impressions of these two people. Lois was articulate and surprisingly poised for such a young woman. Her friendliness had an opaque quality, but Tara wasn't sure whether the woman was hiding something or simply lacked depth.

Raymond Powers was tall, like his son, but heavyset,

and without Chance's spontaneous warmth. A thick white streak slashed his coal-black hair, and Tara suspected he had instructed his hairdresser to create the effect to enhance his dramatic image.

She doubted the man ever did anything without weighing the advantages. Yet she didn't sense any cruelty in him, just the kind of unquestioning self-interest that one might expect from, say, a cat.

"A good businessman never rests on his laurels." Ray was saying to his son as the maid served a tray of appetizers. "Expand or die, that's the watchword of the day."

"Are you thinking of expanding, then?" Chance asked.

Ray and Lois exchanged glances, and Tara gathered that the point had not been raised by accident. "We've got some talks scheduled in a couple of weeks about an acquisition." Raymond leaned back in his easy chair.

"What kind of company?"

"CD-ROM gaming." Ray lit a cigarette and glanced around for an ashtray. Lois handed him one. "It's a wide-open field. Combining our special-effects know-how with their experience in writing and programming games, we could corner a chunk of the market."

"Sounds like a marriage made in heaven," Chance murmured.

"First we have to persuade the lady to say yes, so to speak." Ray inhaled a lungful of smoke. "And reach a prenuptial agreement that's mutually acceptable."

"I see." From his cool tone, Chance must be seeing something that Tara had missed.

"The management of the company plays its cards close to its chest," Raymond said. "I wish they would be more specific about their concerns. As you know, I'm not a mind reader.''

"I'm sure they're telling you as much as they think you need to know," Chance said.

Tara kept getting the impression that there were undercurrents to this conversation. Perhaps that was always the case between parents and their grown children, especially if they didn't get along.

She felt a pang of regret for the estrangement with her own father. She would happily trade his cold rejection for Raymond's manipulations, or whatever he was doing tonight. While there was contact, there was still hope of a reconciliation.

The conversation switched to the state of the economy and then to politics. When the maid announced dinner, they adjourned to the capacious dining room.

The more she thought about it, the less likely it seemed that Lois could afford to live this way on a beginner's salary. Most likely the apartment belonged to Raymond's company, and for some reason he was indulging his young cousin by letting her live there.

Tara didn't get the sense there was anything romantic between the two. Maybe the man simply like helping relatives, or maybe he considered Lois a valuable ally. But in what way?

Once the veal marsala, asparagus and new potatoes had been served and everyone's wineglasses filled, the conversation turned to a recent article about Chance. It had detailed his successes in predicting the stock market.

"It's almost as if he has a sixth sense," Lois told Tara. "You're working with him, so maybe you can tell us. I'm dying to know—how does he do it?"

"Research," Tara said promptly. "Thoroughness. And instinct, I guess. Why don't you ask Chance?"

"He's very closemouthed about his methods." Raymond savored a mouthful of asparagus before continuing. "It's the instinct part that interests me. What kind of instinct? How does it work?"

"Nothing mysterious about it." Chance hardly touched his food, as if he needed to keep all his senses alert. "It's a matter of paying close attention to the news and picking up on trends."

"I could use some of that instinct in my business." The blandness in Ray's tone was belied by the tension in his arm as he reached for his wineglass.

He bumped it, and the glass teetered at a dangerous angle. Tara gasped, certain the purple liquid was about to soak the white linen tablecloth. At the last instant, the cup righted itself, almost in defiance of the laws of gravity.

Ray smiled. "Haven't lost the old touch, have I?"

Lois beamed. Chance shrugged. Tara wondered what on earth the man was talking about.

"The real trick," Ray said, "would be to get inside people's heads. Even exercise a little mind control, which I always thought might be possible if a person applied himself. A person with the right gifts, of course."

"And the wrong ethics," said Chance.

Lois sighed. "I just don't seem to have the family touch."

"For what?" said Tara.

She felt Ray's attention swing toward her, as if he were really seeing her for the first time. "Intuition, as my son calls it. How about you, my dear? Do you pick up feelings from other people, get a sense of how they're likely to act?"

"Not to any unusual degree." Tara wished she didn't feel as if she were on display. The food was delicious, but she could hardly taste it anymore. "Except where my son is concerned, of course. Mothers always have a sixth sense about their children."

A stillness fell over the table, and then Lois said, "My goodness, I didn't realize you were married. My grand-mother said you and Chance— I mean—"

"I'm not married," Tara said.

"Divorced?"

"No." She felt no obligation to elaborate, but it looked as if her hostess were going to pry further.

It was a relief when Ray intervened. "So you have a son. How old is he?"

"Six." Pleased to be on a less touchy subject, Tara said, "He's very bright but mischievous."

"Sounds like he's all boy." Ray nodded his approval. "What sort of mischief does he get into?"

Again, Tara got the feeling she was being questioned for a reason, but what possible interest could these people have in Harry? "Well—"

"Just the usual stuff," Chance said. "He's very inter-ested in softball. Think you might like to come over and toss a ball around sometime, Dad?"

Judging by Raymond's expression of distaste, tossing softballs was not one of his favorite activities.

The maid cleared their dishes and poured coffee. Ray lit another cigarette, and the conversation became general until they were alone with their slices of chocolate cheesecake.

Ray turned to Tara. "Tell me something. Suppose you learned that your son had an unusual ability. Let's say he had a gift for healing, but he refused to use it. Wouldn't you urge him to become a doctor and use that gift?"

"That's not a fair analogy." Chance's mouth tightened. "Healing involves helping people, not taking advantage of them."

This must be the crux of the matter, Tara thought. Raymond wanted his son to apply his instincts to furthering the proposed acquisition. Chance objected to the way his father conducted business and didn't want to let his talents be misused.

"I would certainly discuss the possibilities with my son," she said, "but I'd also listen to what he had to say. Ultimately our children have to follow their own hearts, Mr. Powers, and as parents we need to know when it's time to let go."

A smile softened Chance's face. Warmth flooded Tara as she realized she had said the right thing.

Neither Lois nor Ray appeared satisfied, however, and the conversation lagged. As they said good-night, she gathered the dinner hadn't gone as they hoped.

When she and Chance were in the car, she said, "Your father must hold a very high opinion of you, to bring so much pressure to bear."

"I wish he would take your advice." There was resignation and sadness in his voice. "The man just doesn't know when to quit."

"My father quits too easily," Tara said.

"My mom was the one who quit too easily in our family." Chance's eyes glittered in the dark. "She left when I was a child, completely cut off contact. I don't even know where she is."

"Have you tried to find her?"

He let out a low breath. "No. I respect her privacy. And I suspect my father might have been pressuring her to do something unethical. I just hope she didn't regret giving birth to me."

"What a terrible thought!" Tara couldn't imagine why he would even think such a thing.

"They didn't marry for love," Chance explained. "Tara, listen. My family is unusual. It may be hard to grasp, but I want to come clean with you."

After tonight's uncomfortable dinner with his cousin and father, Tara wasn't sure how much she wanted to hear. Still, she treasured the fact that Chance was taking her into his confidence. "Is it anything like your aunt Cynda and her crystal ball?"

"Quite a bit like that," he agreed.

"Well, if I had a crystal ball, I'd say you were going to hit somebody unless you quit swerving around in your lane," griped the car's computer.

"I wasn't swerving—much," said Chance.

"Look out!" cried the car as the traffic ahead stopped suddenly and Chance had to slam on the brakes. "You see what I mean?"

He turned to Tara. "I'll tell you what. Let's continue this discussion where I don't have to watch out for traffic. There's a whirlpool bath on my private patio. Do you feel like a soak?"

Now that he mentioned it, her shoulders ached from bending over the computer that afternoon. "I'd love it," she said.

LURING TARA into his whirlpool bath by moonlight probably hadn't been the best idea in the world, Chance scolded himself as he stepped out of his bathroom wearing black trunks. He'd been so preoccupied by the conversation at dinner that he hadn't considered the ramifications of getting her alone at night in scanty clothing.

He simply wanted an uninterrupted chance to explain what was going on, and to unwind after that tense dinner.

It was time to take another step toward her acceptance of Harry as he really was.

It troubled him that Ray had learned of the boy's existence. If he knew the truth, he would almost certainly try to subvert Harry's talents to his own advantage. But Chance didn't intend for his father to find out about the boy's parentage.

Tara had come through like a trooper. Even without understanding the subtext of the discussion, she'd given Ray the right answer about letting children choose their own path. Chance wished his father could grasp the principle that other people, including one's offspring, were not objects to be exploited.

He only hoped Lois would stop hero-worshiping his father before she got sucked irrevocably into his way of thinking. Still, she was an adult and had to make her own decisions.

A tap at the door of his suite drew Chance from his reverie. He swallowed hard at the sight of Tara standing there in a one-piece russet swimsuit with a towel tossed over her shoulder.

He didn't need the sight of her to remind him of her inviting shape. His senses were imprinted with every detail of those firm small breasts, the slender waist and the long legs with their slightly angular knees.

What he'd forgotten was the golden sheen of her skin by lamplight and the vulnerability in her face. Then there was the dangerous way his thoughts kept thrusting into her mind. Already he could feel the heat that flared inside her at his nearness.

Drawing on his self-taught discipline, Chance visualized a glass wall forming between the two of them. As he did so, the air abruptly chilled.

Tara took a dazed step backward, her expression as

startled as if a door had slammed in her face. She didn't
seem angry about the sudden withdrawal, however. In
fact, she looked embarrassed. "I keep getting the feeling
I'm dozing off while I'm wide awake. I'll have to make
a point of catching up on my sleep."

"A hot soak ought to relax you." Taking her arm,
Chance guided her through the French doors onto the
shrubbery-enclosed patio.

Touching her made his pulse race, and again he got
the sense of reaching into her mind and seeing through
her eyes. Steam beckoned from the large whirlpool bath,
and the tiles underfoot reminded her of the hotel where
she and her girlfriend had stayed on a weekend trip to
Mexico.

Resolutely, he re-formed the glass wall. Tara shivered.
"I didn't notice how breezy it was."

"The cold makes the pool feel even better," he advised, and switched on the jets.

Dropping her towel, Tara lowered herself into the water and slid down until it reached her chin. Wisps of hair
floated around her like a halo.

Chance caught an image, a far memory, of Tara playing in a forest stream. Sunlight and leaf shadows dappled
her bare breasts as she floated on her back, lazily ges-
turing him to join her. *Not Tara. Ardath.*

He settled into the hot water, as far from her as the
pool allowed. Having an honest chat was going to be
difficult if he kept muddying it up with past lives. For
once, Chance wished he were just an ordinary guy who
could fall in love without a lot of complications.

Except he didn't dare fall in love. Given the unresolved
passions of their previous existence, there was no telling
what might result. Their goal must be to safeguard their
son's development.

"You may be wondering what my father was getting at tonight," he said.

She shifted, sending ripples stroking up Chance's thighs and right to his masculine center. "I gather he believes in intuition, and particularly in yours."

That had been perceptive of her, he reflected, trying to ignore the way his body responded to her nearness. "Yes, intuition, that's a good name for it. Everyone possesses it to one degree or another."

"But your work is based on keeping track of trends and developments," Tara said. "I guess the subconscious mind makes creative leaps but—"

"There's a lot we don't know about how our minds work." Chance knew he would have a better shot at persuading her if he used logic. "There have always been people who seemed able to predict how others would behave. It's too bad scientists haven't found a reliable way to test their skills."

"Maybe they just pay more attention to the subtle clues that we all give off." She stretched, not seeming to notice how the movement displayed her body to advantage. There was nothing calculated about Tara.

Ironically, Chance realized, he could view her more clearly through this imaginary barrier than when their minds touched. From a distance, he could appreciate her with pure masculine delight, as he would any other woman—or rather, no other woman that he had met. Not in this lifetime, anyway.

Still, he couldn't allow himself to dwell on how much he wanted her. He had an obligation to help Tara understand the new world she had entered that Halloween night seven years ago, the world to which she was now bound irrevocably through her son.

"Scientists tend to discredit what they don't understand," he said. "The West denied for a long time that Eastern mystics could control their heartbeat and blood pressure. Now we routinely use biofeedback to do exactly that."

"So your father thinks intuition can be harnessed?" She frowned. "He believes people can read minds, or even control them? Don't you think that's bizarre?"

"It would certainly be odd by most people's standards," Chance said. "But I know that people can do things that defy scientific principles. The way my father kept his wineglass from tipping over, for example."

She regarded him skeptically. "Oh, come on, Chance. That was just luck."

He searched for a better example, one she could relate to. "How about when Harry turned that fork around in the air?"

Tara stared at him. "How did you know about that? Are you saying you saw us on television before I'd even applied to work for you?"

Darn, he hadn't been thinking clearly. He couldn't admit the whole truth, not yet. If she learned why Chance had really hired her, she would leave at once.

"Harry told me." He hoped that when he finally was able to explain the whole story, she would forgive him this lie.

"Oh!" Even in the moonlight, he could see her flushing. "I'm sorry! I just—but I mean—you didn't actually believe him, did you?"

"He, uh, did make the softball jerk a little in the air," Chance improvised. "Tara, it's rare, but some people do have talents like that."

"Talents?" Steam gave her an ethereal air, but there was nothing misty about the sparks flying from her eyes. "If my son had that kind of power, he'd be a freak!"

He should have anticipated this reaction. Denial was only natural, but he must find a way to break through it. "Don't you suppose the first time a caveman drew an antelope on the wall and it really looked like an antelope, people thought it was frightening? Maybe these are skills we simply don't understand yet."

"I don't buy it," Tara said. "Painting on a cave is nothing like making forks loop around in the air."

He could feel, even through the imaginary glass wall, that she believed more than she wanted to, but was fighting it. He didn't want to shake her sense of security. She needed to take these insights one step at a time, and they'd gone far enough for one night.

"Well, it's an interesting subject." Chance drew himself up into the night air, which promptly turned his skin into a mass of goose bumps. "We'd better get some rest before we both doze off and drown."

"You're right." Following his example, she emerged from the pool. "This water is terrific. And I enjoyed meeting your father and Lois tonight. They're complicated people."

"A little too complicated." He tried not to stare as she stood with one leg propped on the raised edge of the pool, drying herself. In the moonlight, her legs were long and slender, her hips curved and inviting.

"I can't see them getting the best of you, in anything." Tara glanced at him admiringly, and then caught her breath as their eyes met.

In that instant, he saw both Tara and Ardath staring at him. He felt his modern self fade, replaced by a man of the forest who wanted this woman and intended to take her.

The glass wall cracked into tiny chips that glittered like

stars. A sparkling haze enveloped them both, and drew them close.

Chance's hands framed Tara's waist and slid down the silky fabric to the velvet of her skin. Her eyes drifted shut and she curved against him, and in that moment he no longer knew where they were, or even who they were.

Their mouths fit together as if completing a circuit. Energy charged through him. His tongue teased hers, and she pulled him hard against her.

A desperate awareness surged through him, a primitive need to unite them in flesh as well as spirit. There was no space in him for caution; his blood had become a river of flame.

Tara melted into him, nipping lightly at his mouth, urging him to claim her. Her breasts teased his chest, and he could feel the heat of her molten core.

She doesn't know what she's doing. She isn't herself.

He didn't want to hear Chance's voice. He wanted to be Valdemar, savage and remoreseless, seizing what he wanted and willing to die if necessary to keep it.

You don't have the right to make that decision. Tara needs to understand, and so far, she doesn't.

With a deep inner wrench, he pulled away. As soon as the connection broke, Tara shivered in confusion.

Hating himself for doing it, Chance eased back into her mind and conjured a curtain of mist to shield her from the memory of what had just passed between them. It was, he told himself, a form of protection.

Dazed, she wrapped a towel around her shoulders and said good-night. As he escorted her out, Chance fought down the urge to take her in his arms, kiss her sleepy face and reawaken the sparks he had done his best to extinguish.

His body ached, and after she left he spent long, stinging minutes in an ice-cold shower. It didn't help to remind himself that he deserved this.

HARRY HAD FALLEN ASLEEP with his arms around his favorite teddy bear. Curled under the covers, he reminded Tara of Christopher Robin, forever a child in the Forest.

It was hard to imagine that someday he would grow up. But as she had pointed out to Raymond tonight, eventually each child emerged from the cocoon to make his own way in the world.

When he did, she hoped Harry would be like Chance—sensitive, intelligent and...

And what? Masculine, she thought. Tonight, the man had dominated the darkness, his eyes gleaming in the moonlight, his body taut and ready to burst through the wisp of fabric around his waist.

Tara's body tingled and she realized to her embarrassment that the sight of her boss in a swimsuit had excited her. Had he been aware of it? With all her heart, she hoped not, but there was little that escaped his awareness.

No more moonlight dips in the spa, she told herself firmly, and went to change for bed.

Chapter Eight

"But the other kids still don't like Al." Harry's gray eyes widened with six-year-old sincerity.

"Did you try what I suggested?" Chance said as they finished their hamburgers. Around them, kids were racing toward the restaurant's play area, but Harry considered such activities boring.

"Yeah, I spent recess yesterday showing him how to hit, but he just doesn't get it," the boy said. "Why can't I give his thoughts a little push? I could make him understand!"

"I've explained—"

"Just a little bit!" said Harry.

Chance tried not to show his dismay. His own psi abilities had matured when he was considerably older, and even so it had taken years to master them. Now his son was showing the same talent, but much earlier and without the maturity to understand the issues.

It was lucky he had discovered the boy's existence before things went haywire. Even now, he wondered if the boy could muster the self-discipline to reject the temptations he was encountering.

"You could make things worse," he warned. "In any

case, Al needs to find his own solutions without you monkeying around in his brain.''

"I can't help it," the boy protested. "Sometimes I hear what people are thinking when I don't even want to!''

"I know it must be frustrating.'' It was hard to reason with a six-year-old, although, Chance reflected ruefully, no harder than reasoning with his sixty-year-old father. "But you have to keep working at it.''

"Like I knew the substitute yesterday wasn't going to let us watch a videotape like Mrs. Reed promised,'' Harry said. "She was going to hand out boring old work sheets! So I made her think she *had* to let us watch the video or she would get in trouble.''

"Harry!''

"I didn't mean to!'' The little boy drooped before Chance's disapproval. "Honest, it happened before I even realized what I was doing.''

In the week since Tara had moved in, the boy had progressed alarmingly. It was obvious his powers had lain close to the surface, ready to explode.

Chance was beginning to regret taking Harry to the video store last week and encouraging him to anticipate people's choices. It had been a necessary step if the boy were to learn to control his talents instead of letting them control him. But the risk was that Harry's powers would develop even faster than they might otherwise.

"Whenever you start hearing people's thoughts, you need to imagine a barrier—like a wall—forming between you.''

"I don't think I can,'' Harry said.

"Would you like to try?''

"Sure.''

"Finish eating and let's go somewhere quiet, then.''

Along the restaurant aisle, a mother hurried past carrying a tray, with a toddler pulling at her skirt. Instinctively, Chance made the heavy door to the play area swing open ahead of her, in a slow arc as if air pressure had nudged it.

But he didn't see, until too late, the puddle of spilled soda on the floor. "Oops!" said Harry a split second later, as the woman's foot came down in it.

The tray went flying, the woman staggered against their table and the toddler trotted directly into the path of the thick door as it swung shut.

Both Chance and Harry must have tried to stop the door at the same time, from different angles. With a great crack, the glass split in jagged segments, spraying the floor with shards. It was pure luck that the toddler halted a few inches on the safe side of the threshold.

Everything happened so fast, Chance realized as he helped the woman right herself, that no one else noticed the exact sequence. A restaurant worker and several patrons rushed to the child, exclaiming in surprise at finding him uninjured when he had apparently been struck by the door with shattering force.

Harry frowned. "What went wrong?"

"Sometimes two heads aren't better than one," Chance observed as the woman ran to hug her child. "But it proves my point, doesn't it? Interfering can make things worse. It's not our job to run other people's lives."

The boy made a face. "Yeah, I guess you're right. But I wish I could help Al."

"I suspect that being his friend is a very big help," Chance said. "Want to go to the park and make little waves in the pond?" It was a good visualization exercise, just what the boy needed.

Harry's dubious expression vanished. "Yeah! We can

make the toy boats sail faster! And tickle the ducks' be-hinds!''

He jumped up, ready for action. Chance found himself grinning as he uncoiled from his too-small seat.

Tickling the ducks' bottoms sounded like fun.

TARA HAD WORKED LATE Monday night, helping Chance review the latest economic reports. It was a relief to have Tuesday morning off, while her seemingly tireless employer headed for the office.

After a week on the job, she was beginning to settle in. A person could definitely feel at home here, she reflected as she stretched lazily in bed, watching the clock tick past 9:00 a.m.

Chance had taken Harry to school, another sign of the pair's growing closeness. Seeing them spend so much time together made her vaguely uneasy, knowing that this relationship would be only temporary. Yet she couldn't deny that her son was thirstily soaking up the male attention.

Boys needed fathers, she thought. Of course, plenty of mothers raised their children alone and did a terrific job, just as Tara intended to do.

But being a single mom sometimes reminded her of what it had been like when she was younger and drove a rickety car whose rearview mirror had fallen off. She'd managed, but there was always the sense of something missing.

Tara chuckled. Men were hardly the same as rearview mirrors.

As she showered and dressed, she recalled how Chance had looked last week in his slim trunks, reclining in the whirlpool bath. More than his muscular chest and com-

manding presence, she'd been drawn by the silver gleam
in his eyes.

This weekend, although they'd gone their separate
ways outside of mealtimes, she'd noticed occasional sideways glances from the man as if there were some kind
of link between them. Could he be considering his aunt's
nonsense about past lives?

Toweling off, she wondered exactly how far Chance's
faith in intuition reached. He'd certainly made a point of
discussing it in the hot tub.

How could such a down-to-earth man believe in the
supernatural? But perhaps he hadn't really meant ESP
and psychic phenomena, but rather some form of New
Age spirituality.

With relief, Tara embraced that possibility. Slipping
into jeans and a short cotton sweater, she admitted silently that this enigmatic side of Chance had worried her,
for reasons she couldn't grasp.

But spirituality was another matter. Tara wasn't reli-
gious but she respected those who were, and hoped that
someday she would experience a deeper faith herself.
Perhaps Chance had been referring to theology and she'd
failed to grasp his meaning.

That comforting conclusion enhanced her appetite, and
she took the shortest route to the kitchen, through the
courtyard. Vareena, who had today off from her convenience store clerking job, was playing the boom box at
a low volume and practicing dance steps by herself.

"Only six weeks until the contest!" she called as Tara
went by. "We must not waste a moment!"

Such dedication was commendable, Tara thought as
she slipped into the opposite wing of the house. She
hoped she could watch Rajeev and Vareena compete.
Even if they didn't win, she wanted to cheer them on.

The coffeemaker on the kitchen counter was half-full, and she fixed herself two slices of toast. "We're a little low on eggs but there's enough for an omelet," advised the house computer. It rarely spoke unless addressed but seemed to take a proprietary interest in the kitchen.

"Have you decided on a name yet?" Tara asked.

"I'm considering *Ma Maison* and *Mi Casa*," said the nasal voice. "Although they do make me sound like a restaurant, don't you think? I'm looking for something familiar but with a touch of grandeur."

"How about the *Starship Enterprise?*" Tara suggested.

"There's no need for sarcasm." The computer signed off with an indignant beep.

After breakfast, Tara decided to read the newspaper in the courtyard and soak up some sunshine. Vareena had vanished, and the open space sat quiet in the morning light.

Stepping out, she let the rays wash over her face. She always felt at home out here, surrounded by the house and yet in touch with the sky and the wind.

Springtime flowers—pansies and poppies and petunias—overflowed the small planters. The fountain sprang to life as she came near, its twin sprays fanning and swirling in an everchanging design.

A padded bench provided a place to sit facing the rear of the house. Although she had intended to read the paper, Tara let herself float in a sunny mental haze.

Even out here, she caught an almost subliminal whiff of the scent that pervaded the house—masculinity touched with the essence of herbs. She seemed to remember it from long ago.

Long ago, right here.

Blinking against the sunshine, she stared at the curving

stairway the led to the second-floor balcony. Since moving in, she hadn't given much thought to what might lie in the tower, but now it whispered of wonderful secrets.

She had no business entering Chance's private rooms, Tara scolded herself sternly. On the other hand, he hadn't said that she couldn't look around the house.

Without realizing she was rising, she moved toward the stairs. What harm could it do to explore?

In the back of her mind, Tara noted that something was amiss. This odd, sleeplike state shouldn't be seizing her in the middle of the day. It was as if she walked through a dream, a dream that she had experienced before.

None of it made sense, but the tower room was calling. All things would be explained, once she arrived.

Up the stairs Tara glided, and onto the balcony. The doorknob to the tower room turned easily in her hand and she went in.

Disappointment quivered through her. There was nothing here, just a round room with a polished wooden floor. Not even furniture.

"House?" she ventured. "What is this place?"

"What would you like it to be?" said the house. "A bedchamber? An office? He's stashed all kinds of things in the walls."

"In the walls?" Tara noted for the first time that the walls were pierced by thin cracks outlining rectangles and other shapes. "How about a bedroom?"

From the rear wall descended a bed with a soft covering. Panels slid open on the walls, revealing an oak dresser. Velvet curtains, which had been hidden within a valance, lowered themselves across the windows.

She remembered this place, and a man too. The name

that came to mind was not a name, though, but a description: the Magician.

A mask covered his face but the eyes glowed silver as they bored into hers. Shudders ran through Tara. Something held her transfixed, half in dream and half in wakefulness, bathing in partially remembered details and trembling with the impossibility of it.

"Isn't this clever?" chattered the house. "Would you like to see the office?"

"No, thank you." Numbly, Tara stumbled out onto the balcony. She *had* been to this house before. It wasn't from a scene from a movie, or a trick of the mind. And that figure in the black cloak and mask... She did know him. She knew him intimately.

Thank goodness for the heat of the day, soothing her shaken spirit so she could think more clearly. What exactly had happened here, and what did it have to do with Chance?

Before she could sort out her jumbled impressions, Rajeev hurried into the courtyard. "Miss Blayne?" he said. "Ah, the school has called regarding your son."

"Is he all right?" She went down the stairs at a rapid clip.

"It seems that he is well," said Rajeev. "But as for the school itself, who can say?"

HARRY WISHED he could wipe the alarm and confusion from his mother's face. Things really weren't so bad, but that was hard to prove, with the principal soaked to the skin, the leaves blasted off a bush in front of the school and the fire captain turning three shades of red.

"There wasn't any *real* damage," he protested as Mom knelt on the floor to bring her face level with his.

A bunch of other people stood around the front office, glaring at him.

"But there could have been," she said. "The principal says you climbed into the fire truck and turned on the hose. Is that right?"

"No!" Harry started to get mad. Grown-ups shouldn't tell lies, especially about little kids. "Where's Chance? He'd understand."

"I'm the one who needs to understand." His mother wiped a wisp of hair from her forehead. "Now let's see. The fire fighters were visiting for Fire Prevention Week, and the kids were checking out the fire truck. Then what?"

It was hard, he discovered as he talked, to explain this stuff. Mom couldn't seem to grasp the obvious, like why Harry had persuaded Al to climb into the cab and turn on the siren.

"It made him a hero!" he explained with all the patience he could muster. "The kids were, like, 'Wow!' And I did talk him into it, Mom. I didn't *make* him do it."

"Then what?" she asked wearily.

This was going to be tough to get across. Nobody had believed him so far.

In fact, they'd gotten so confused that the fire captain was swearing it had been Harry in the cab and not Al. What made it even more complicated was that Harry felt he ought to take the blame, because in a way he *was* responsible.

"Well, the captain started to grab Al, so I thought, what if he thought there really was a fire? Then Al would be a hero for sounding the siren, right?"

"Keep going," said his mother.

"So I—" Harry took a deep breath. "I know Chance

said I shouldn't, but I put this idea in the captain's mind. Like that the front of the school was on fire. He started shouting to the other guys to hook up the hoses, and then, wham! There was water everywhere! They even got the principal!" It had been awesome. "Only, they're kind of mad now."

"Honey, you couldn't have put an idea in the captain's mind." Mom let out a sigh. "You have to tell me the truth."

"It is the truth! Ask Chance!"

"What's he got to do with this?" She wore a tight, unhappy expression that scared Harry a little.

"He's been helping me. You know how I made the fork turn around in the air? Well, I can do other stuff, too. Really neat stuff with people's minds, but Chance says I shouldn't. He can explain it better than I can."

She shook her head. "I can't sort this out right now, Harry. I certainly can't contradict a fire captain who was an eyewitness."

She stood up, and Harry felt as if he were stranded on Mars with his last link to Earth cut off.

He heard his mother apologizing to the other grown-ups. Then the principal said the word *suspended* a couple of times and gave his mother a paper to sign.

Finally, Mom took Harry's hand and led him out of the office to her car. He turned toward the school yard and saw his classmates lining up for lunch. Two of the kids were fighting over who got to stand next to Al.

At least he'd done some good today.

ON THE DRIVE HOME, Tara couldn't begin to make sense of what had happened. Why was Harry lying to her, and what did Chance have to do with it?

Her son's muddled explanation kept getting mixed up

with the strange feelings she'd experienced in the tower room. She couldn't stop thinking about Chance's words a few nights earlier: *People can do things that defy scientific principles.*

Had he been conducting experiments with her son? It was unthinkable.

Then she nearly couldn't find the house. For some reason, she kept wanting to turn left where she should have turned right. It was Harry who pointed out the landmarks and got her headed in the right direction.

With mixed feelings, Tara pulled into the driveway and saw Chance's car sitting in the open, as if he'd been in too great a hurry to put it in the garage. Was something wrong at work? She didn't think she could handle another crisis at the moment.

The front door stood open. With Harry on her heels, she hurried through the living room and into the courtyard.

She was heading toward the rear office when she saw Chance standing on the curved stairs, as if he'd just emerged from the tower. Anger flashed from his eyes.

"What were you doing up here?" he demanded. "The computer beeped me. It's programmed to do that when anyone enters the tower."

"I didn't know it was off-limits." The way he held himself, erect and imposing, rang bells in her mind. He had stood this way before, and she had watched him from this angle. Unable to pinpoint the memory, Tara rushed on. "Harry got into trouble at school. He claims you were working with him on some kind of—of mind games."

Chance's anger turned cold. "Harry?"

"I didn't mean to!" the boy blurted. "Honest, I didn't. I just talked Al into turning on the siren and he was going to get in trouble so I made the fireman think the school was on fire! That's all.''

"What's he talking about, 'making' the fireman think something?" Tara gritted her teeth with impatience as Chance descended the stairs.

He regarded her assessingly, his gaze hooded. Mistrust flooded through her. Always before, the man had struck her as frank and honest, but now she saw only calculation in his manner.

He *was* up to something. But what on earth could it have to do with her son?

"Harry," Chance said, "if you'll go into my private den, there's a new video game you can play. Your mother and I need to talk."

The boy brightened. "Cool! Now that I'm suspended, I'll have lots of time to play!"

"Suspended?" Chance said.

"Go on, Harry." Tara shooed him away. "Mr. Powers is right. We do have a lot to talk about."

They went into the office. Its windowed length was flooded with sunlight, but today it seemed full of shadows.

Sitting stiffly in a straight-backed chair, Tara recounted the morning's events. She expected Chance to dismiss her son's story, but he listened with resignation.

"Something like this was bound to happen," he said when she finished.

"Something like what?"

"The boy's gifted, Tara. Remember those special abilities we were talking about? I know you don't want to believe in them, but for Harry's sake you must."

She gripped the arms of the chair, fighting a wave of disbelief. There were no such special talents, whether they involved making forks dodge in midair or planting hallucinations in people's minds.

"I believe one thing," she said. "You've been putting ideas in my son's head. What were you doing, working with him behind my back? All the time you made me think you cared about him."

"I do." Chance leaned forward on the couch. "I was trying to break the news gently because I knew it would be hard to accept."

"What news?" she said.

His jaw worked, and she could see he was choosing his words with care. "My hiring you wasn't entirely a coincidence."

"You did see him on television!" The man's duplicity took her breath away. He lived in a beautiful house and spoke soothing words, he was respected and admired by his entire staff, but he'd been using her to get to Harry. "You imagined he had some hidden talents and you wanted to subvert them!"

"No!" The denial rasped from him. "Just the opposite, Tara! I want to protect him and teach him how to control his ability. If I don't, someone like my father *will* exploit him."

She stood up, hoping he couldn't see her hands trembling. "We have to leave. I can't trust you around my son anymore. He has no magical abilities, but for some reason that I can't fathom, you believe he does. He's just an ordinary little boy with a vivid imagination."

"He does have gifts, and they're going to create more trouble if he doesn't learn to harness them," Chance said.

"Why do you keep insisting on this?" Tears threatened to wreck her composure, but Tara pressed on. "It's outrageous! Just leave us alone!"

"I can't leave you alone," he said. "I'm responsible for Harry. I'm his father."

A chill robbed her of movement. She couldn't even shout a denial, because, incredibly, his claim made sense.

That was why she kept remembering this house and the courtyard and the tower. Chance was the Magician. For some perverse reason, he believed he really could work sorcery, and so could his son.

His son. Fury and pain raged inside her. After all these years, how dare he come forward?

He had seduced her and then made no attempt to find her again. Nor had she tried to find him, but that was because her memory had been so clouded and confused.

What had Chance done to her that night? She hadn't felt drugged, exactly, but rather as if—as if—

As if he were controlling my mind.

The possibility frightened her more than anything that had happened today. Tara took a step toward the door. "You have no right to him," she said. "I won't let you have him."

"I have no intention of seeking custody." Through his grim expression shone a hint of concern, but she knew it must be feigned. "I only want to help him. And you. Tara, I'm sorry I haven't been around all these years. I didn't know he existed until I saw him on television."

"Well, forget you ever found out," she snapped. "Forget you ever met us!"

Then she ran for the door before she could embarrass herself by breaking into tears.

CHANCE'S HANDS CLENCHED as he listened to the sounds of departure. Tara had packed in record time and was now dragging her protesting son out of the house as if the forces of evil were right behind them.

When Rajeev peered into the room questioningly, Chance shook his head. They couldn't stop Tara, not today. Catching his glower, the housekeeper beat a swift retreat.

His son's future was the most important matter Chance would ever confront, but he must not let his concern overwhelm his judgment. He couldn't let himself think about Tara and how much he wanted to hold her again, either.

In the short run, it might be possible to touch her mind and make her stay. But to manipulate her would be to prove himself unworthy, and to ruin any possibility of a lasting relationship with his son.

For now, he had to let her go. Bringing her back would test every ounce of his self-restraint, but he was going to do it fair and square.

Chapter Nine

Tara circled a classified ad on the paper spread across Denise's kitchen table. It didn't give a company name, just a post office box.

"I'm getting to the point where I don't trust anyone," she admitted to her friend, who was stirring a pot of spaghetti. "How do I know Chance didn't place this ad just to lure me back?"

"It's only been two days. He wouldn't have had time to get it in the paper," Denise pointed out, shoving a strand of red hair behind her ear.

Tara glanced across the tiny kitchen to the living room, where Harry lay on the couch studying his favorite picture book. Had it really only been two days since she'd stalked out of *Ma Maison,* or *Mi Casa,* or whatever name the house had decided on?

It seemed much longer. With Harry suspended from school, it was difficult to seek work. Her problem would be compounded by the fact that she had left her most recent job abruptly.

Thank goodness for Denise. Otherwise, Tara didn't know where she would have gone. But she couldn't presume on her friend's hospitality for too long.

"If I haven't found a job by the time Harry's back in

school, I'm going to apply to a temporary agency," she said.

"I've got a better idea." Denise emptied a jar of spaghetti sauce into a microwave casserole. "Chance is rich, isn't he? Sue him for child support."

Tara shuddered. "He said he wouldn't seek custody, but if I sue him, he might change his mind." She lowered her voice. "I don't even want Harry to find out who his father is."

"If he had any honor, he'd send you money without being asked," asserted her friend.

"He did." A check for several hundred dollars in severance pay had arrived by messenger that morning, with a note indicating that Chance's lawyer would be drawing up a trust fund for Harry. "I don't want to take it, though. It means maintaining a link with him."

Tara hadn't even intended to reveal where she was going, but Vareena had insisted on getting the address in case any possessions were left behind. Knowing how children managed to lose toys under cushions and behind furniture, Tara had reluctantly agreed.

She knew, of course, that sooner or later she would have to tell her son the truth. But the older he got, the firmer a grip he would have on reality, and the better able he would be to reject this nonsense about magic.

From the refrigerator, Denise fetched a bag of salad mix and poured it into a bowl. "I'm not sure you can avoid contact. The way this guy believes in hocus-pocus, he's probably trying to work a Vulcan mind-meld over the telephone lines. You really found yourself a doozy, kid."

In the living room, Harry let his book fall to the floor and sprawled across the sofa, his little face a picture of misery. "When are we going back to Chance's house?" he whined. "I miss him, Mommy."

"'How sharper than a serpent's tooth it is/ To have a thankless child!'" Tara was surprised she recalled the line so clearly; she must have memorized it in high school. "Isn't that Shakespeare?"

"Beats me." Denise poured the spaghetti into a strainer. Tara got up to set the table. "Hey, you did everything last night. It's my turn!"

"There's two of us and one of you," Tara pointed out. "The least I can do is set out the plates." A sharp buzz at the door startled her. "Were you expecting anyone?"

Setting the colander on the counter, Denise pointed her forefingers at her temples and made a high-pitched "woo-woo" noise. "I'm getting a picture now. Someone is in the hall. It is either a man or a woman. He is short or she is fat. How am I doing?"

Before Tara could answer, Harry flung the door open. After a brief, disappointed pause, she heard her son say, "Who're you?"

Please don't let it be a lawyer, thought Tara as she hurried into the living room.

To her astonishment, the woman standing there was Lois Powers, sleek and dressed for success in a navy linen suit and pin-striped blouse. "Hi! I'm not intruding, am I?"

Tara's first notion was that Chance had enlisted his cousin to try to win her back, but she dismissed that idea almost at once. He would have chosen Rajeev or Vareena, not someone allied with his father. "Please come in. What can I do for you?"

The young woman stepped inside, her dark eyes flicking across the worn furniture and outdated carpet. The decor was a painful contrast to her own penthouse, Tara supposed, and wondered why she felt so defensive.

"I dropped by Chance's house, and Rajeev told me you'd left." Lois flashed a smile that seemed a trifle forced. "When I told Raymond, he was curious to know what had happened. Although they don't spend much time together, he's always concerned about his son."

Warning alarms sounded in Tara's brain. Most likely Lois intended to pump her for information about Chance's business dealings and perhaps learn more about his supposed intuition.

The danger was that Lois and Ray, who for some incomprehensible reason appeared to believe in magic, might find out that Harry was Chance's son. If they did, what would they try to do with that information?

"There's nothing to be concerned about," Tara said. "We didn't work well together after all. I don't mean to be inhospitable, Lois, but we were about to eat."

"You could join us," piped Denise from the doorway. Tara wished that she'd briefed her friend better on the eccentricities of Chance's relatives.

She couldn't avoid introducing the two women, and the next thing she knew they were all scrunched around the small table, downing their spaghetti and salad. Or rather, three of them ate with gusto while Lois picked at her food.

"You're Chance's cousin?" Harry asked. "Can you do—"

"Harry!" Tara didn't dare allow her son to finish that sentence. "You haven't touched your salad."

"It needs more dressing," he protested.

As Tara tapped out some more, Lois said, "Chance is a cool guy, isn't he, Harry? Did he ever show you any tricks?"

"He can make funny waves in the pond, and one of the ducks kept ruffling its wings like he was tickling its bottom!" the boy said through a mouthful of spaghetti. "I can do it, too!"

"You can?" Lois asked.

"By throwing pebbles," Tara interjected. "Isn't that right, son?"

"Mommy, I'm not supposed to tell lies."

"That's exactly my point."

Making a face, her son began picking the shredded carrots out of his salad.

To Tara's relief, Denise launched into a description of a moisturizer that she swore would give Lois's hair even more sheen. She also suggested a perm to add body, and soon the two were deep into a discussion of a new process for strengthening fingernails.

Obviously, Denise had grasped the fact that Lois was as hooked as her cousin on the subject of mental powers. Being a beautician provided a convenient means of distracting their guest, for which Tara was grateful.

As soon as he finished eating, Harry cleared his place and retreated to the bedroom to watch television. Tara felt herself relax for the first time since Lois had arrived.

"I'll drop by your salon and get some of that moisturizer," the dark-haired woman promised as she set aside her napkin. "Now I'm afraid I've got to run. I'm glad to see you're all right, Tara, although I suspect Chance didn't treat you very well. He's a selfish man, you know."

Denise accompanied them to the front door. "At least he's going to set up a trust fund."

"Excuse me?"

Tara tried to shoot her friend a warning look, but De-

nise didn't notice. "Well, because of his being Harry's—"
She stopped, finally realizing she'd said too much.

"Harry's what?" Lois took in Denise's dismay and
Tara's alarm. "Wait a minute. When Harry was talking
about making waves in the pond, he wasn't kidding. He's
Chance's kid, isn't he? How did that happen?"

"In the usual way." This was getting messier by the
minute.

"I'll bet you have a very unusual little boy there."
Lois glanced toward the bedroom. "Does he know he's
got a grandfather and a whole bunch of other relatives?"

"He doesn't even know he's got a father, and you're
not going to tell him," Tara growled. "I don't want to
be rude, Lois, but there are some matters that simply
don't concern you *or* Raymond Powers. My son belongs
to me. Period."

"Well, of course." Lois couldn't repress a hint of
smugness in her smile. "Denise, thanks so much for dinner and the beauty tips. I'll be going now."

As soon as the door closed behind her, Tara collapsed
on the sofa. "I'm sorry," moaned Denise. "I didn't realize it was so touchy."

"Just promise me you won't let her anywhere near
Harry when I'm not around."

Denise's eyes narrowed as if she were facing an enemy. "I'll chop her nails into nubs and dye her hair orange. But what would she do with him?"

"I have no idea," Tara admitted. "That whole family
is crazy."

HALDEN OF THE FAR VISION hadn't led a very happy life,
Chance reflected as he snapped shut the aging volume.
He was glad at least that the sad story had kept him
distracted for part of an evening.

It was Thursday night and Tara had been gone for two days. Two days and seven hours, to be exact.

During that time, Chance had worked hard, giving his clients the concentration they deserved but afterward remembering nothing of what he'd done.

He had rented two movies and watched neither. Sat in front of his new video game and failed to make heads or tails of the tumbling figures. Eaten a viciously spicy dish of Rajeev's by mistake, and nearly had to undergo a stomach transplant.

The one thing he would not do was to interfere with Tara's life until enough time had passed for her anger to wane. Clearly, he would have to approach her with great care and restraint.

What he wanted to do was drive over to Denise's apartment and beg, demand, cajole and exhort Tara to forgive him. But to do so might inspire her to flee the area entirely.

Chance's attention returned to the book on his desk. Poor Halden had turned out to be a kind of Cassandra, able to foretell the future but unappreciated by those he advised.

One nobleman, told that he would contract a disease if he didn't stop taking mistresses, had tried to burn the man at the stake when the prophecy proved true. It hadn't been much of a prophecy, really, Chance thought, since the likelihood of contracting a disease in those days must have been overwhelming.

The leader of a rebellion, informed that he would lose both a battle and his head, went after Halden with a pickax. Only, the mysterious appearance of a lightning bolt had frightened the attacker away.

Had Halden planted a hallucination in the rebel's

mind? The book didn't say. It didn't explain whether the prophecy about losing his head had come true, either.

Frustrated, Chance strode from the tower, the book clamped under his arm. He'd skimmed the thing from back to front, but without dates or many recognizable place names, he had a hard time accepting it as anything more than a collection of myths.

Yet if Valdemar and Ardath were imaginary, why had he experienced such a vivid memory of perishing in a fire? He reminded himself that even a stopped clock was right twice a day, so maybe the book had gotten a few things correct.

In any event, he felt a strong urge to return it to Aunt Cynda. So strong an urge, he realized, that she must be summoning him. Couldn't she just use the telephone once in a while?

The evening was pleasant, the spring air crisp and touched with promise. Chance might have enjoyed the drive if his car hadn't reminded him at least three times that it needed a tune-up.

Aunt Cynda answered the door on the first knock. She regarded the book with a frown. "I didn't send for you because I wanted this back. You can study it as long as you like."

Chance followed her into the cluttered room and set the book on a table. "I'm done with it."

"Men! Always impatient." She settled onto a velour love seat.

"Does the reason you want to see me have anything to do with past lives?" He felt too restless to sit, so he leaned against a high-backed wing chair. "Or have you seen something in your crystal ball?"

Aunt Cynda had tried for most of her life to predict the future, with unimpressive results. She certainly hadn't inherited Halden's far-seeing. But, Chance reflected, there was a first time for everything.

"Past lives! Fortune-telling! Pooh!" she said. "My granddaughter was here this afternoon and I heard it right from her lips that you have a son. A son! Imagine! You didn't even tell me! How am I supposed to keep the genealogical records up-to-date?"

Chance stared at her. How could Lois know about Harry? "How did she find out?"

"She said she went to see Tara and that girlfriend of hers mentioned something about a trust fund," snapped his great-aunt. "How long did you plan to keep this a secret?"

Tara had barely moved out of his house, and already she and Harry were in danger. Although he didn't think his father would intentionally harm either of them, Ray was likely to act first and think later when he had a major business deal at stake.

"Aunt Cynda, I didn't want my father to know," Chance said. "I wasn't trying to keep it from you."

Understanding softened the elder lady's face. "That does make sense. He hasn't been good for Lois, and he won't be good for your boy, either. Can't you work your mind control on him, for goodness' sake? Give the man some ethics!"

It would have been a tempting thought had such a thing been possible. "I can't change anybody permanently," Chance said. "Besides, Ray's got enough ability of his own that he'd be able to block me."

He began pacing, a difficult task in such a crowded apartment. Vases, magazine racks, umbrella stands and chair legs kept conspiring to bang his shins.

"Well, get her back!" said Aunt Cynda. "Under your protection."

"She doesn't even believe in magic. She certainly doesn't believe in me," he muttered.

"Make her believe! You can do it, if anyone can. You're the only one in the family with any *real* talent."

It went against Chance's instincts to take a direct approach. He was as likely to antagonize Tara as to persuade her. But what choice did he have?

TARA EMERGED from the dentist's office onto a side street in Westwood to discover that it was raining.

Los Angeles rarely got much rain after the middle of April, and it was now the beginning of May. Yet the drizzle was thickening into a downpour.

The interview had been a mess, with the dentist trying to talk to her in between fitting a crown and filling a cavity. He wanted a receptionist with experience in the medical field, and despite the fact that Tara was more than qualified to make appointments and handle billing, he hadn't seemed impressed.

She had another interview scheduled a few blocks away in an hour. There was no time to go home for lunch, but she couldn't justify paying the steep prices at one of the trendy eateries in this upscale area near U.C.L.A.

With a sigh, Tara decided to duck into a restaurant nearby and nurse a cup of tea as long as possible. If she were lucky, the rain might let up before her next interview.

Staring out the open door of the professional building, she watched passing students laugh as the rain soaked their long hair. Had she ever been that carefree?

Having a child had changed everything. Not that she would trade Harry for all the freedom in the world, but Tara wished she didn't always have to struggle so hard. And right now she wished she had an umbrella.

Deciding she'd lurked in the entranceway long enough, she stepped out onto the sidewalk. Before more than a few drops could pelt her hair, however, an umbrella appeared in her hand as if by magic.

It didn't exactly appear; rather, it floated there from across the street, or so it seemed to Tara. She'd only caught an impression of movement from the corner of her eye, and she knew that impression couldn't be accurate.

The umbrella was an attractive shade of dark blue, with an ivory handle. The construction was sturdy, and the panels already unfurled.

If someone had thrown it toward her, it would have spun around and landed after only a few feet. Nor was there a strong wind that might have carried it in her direction.

From beneath its protection, she peered about for the owner. She saw him at once, standing on the sidewalk opposite, in front of a bookshop.

Chance Powers gave her a lopsided grin, mischief sparkling in his silver eyes. A gust of rain-laced wind ruffled his dark hair, but he didn't appear to notice.

He looked solid and safe, standing there in his camel-hair raincoat and dark slacks. An impulse twitched at Tara, to cross the street and nestle into the shelter of those broad shoulders and strong arms.

Behind him in the display window, she noticed posters advertising New Age books. The banner read Put A Little Magic In Your Life.

It seemed the man had the power to conjure shop windows to suit his purpose, and to levitate umbrellas. She could almost believe the rain itself had been summoned at his command.

What was she thinking? This wasn't sorcery but trickery. Tara stared accusingly at the umbrella, but there were no strings attached. Not the literal kind, anyway.

But Chance hadn't stumbled into her path by accident. He was too busy a man to be wandering around Westwood in the middle of the day.

He must have tracked her down, probably to try to talk her into letting him see Harry. Well, it wouldn't work.

As for the umbrella, she hadn't figured out how he had transported it across the street, but if he didn't find a similar means of snatching it back, she was going to keep it. Until the rain stopped, anyway.

The streets in Westwood ran at sharp angles to each other, which made for jumbled traffic but interesting visuals. Now that she had an umbrella, Tara decided to walk two blocks to a café near the accounting office where she had her second appointment. She enjoyed walking in the rain, as long as it didn't require getting soaked.

As she ambled down the street, Chance loitered in front of the bookstore, taking an interest in the contents of the window. Tara hoped he was giving up on her, but she doubted it.

Sure enough, a minute later he began strolling on a parallel course, past boutiques and jewelry stores. His stride had a jaunty spring to it, as if he were a young adventurer in Paris to seek his fortune.

Tara had never been to France, but she imagined the City of Lights might look like this in the rain. The clear colors of shops and passersby blurred into an Impressionist canvas, brightened by a hint of sunlight sifting through the clouds.

As she waited at a signal, she saw Chance stop before a flower stand and purchase a splash of scarlet. She wondered if he were going to waft it, too, her way, but instead he stuck the carnation into the top buttonhole of his rain-coat.

The pedestrian light shifted to the symbol for Walk, and Tara was about to step from the curb when a car gunned its way around the corner, swishing through a pool of water. Off balance, she struggled to hold her place on the sidewalk, and only too late saw the spray fanning toward her.

In the instant before it hit, she knew she was going to be drenched. With no time to change, she would arrive at her job interview looking like a drowned rat.

With a splat, the water struck. Tara blinked. She'd been anticipating the slushy sensation so sharply that her skin went cold, but she wasn't wet.

Water dripped in midair, as if spattered across a sheet of Plexiglas. Around her, people stared at the rectangular blur directly in front of her, until it trembled and vanished.

Across the street, Chance inclined his head as if taking a bow. She had the impression he was tipping his hat, except that he wasn't wearing one.

Tara decided her hunger pangs must be getting the better of her. She should have planned ahead and brought a sandwich, but this morning she'd been too nervous to have an appetite.

In the next block, she spotted the café with its rainbow awning. Grateful for the refuge, Tara hurried inside, furling her umbrella.

A waiter seated her near the window and handed her an embossed menu. Around her, women in stylish dresses and men in casually elegant suits were filling up the tables.

Examining the offerings, Tara felt her heart sink. She'd almost convinced herself to splurge a little, but even the simplest sandwich cost enough to feed her and Harry for several days.

As if that weren't frustrating enough, a dessert cart sat nearby, piled with pastries, cheesecake, mousse cake, carrot cake, flan and an immense cream puff topped with chocolate sauce and a cherry. Tara was willing to guess each slice cost as much as a sandwich, or close to it.

Reining in her yearnings, she resolutely ordered tea. The waiter ran down a list of varieties, caffeinated and decaf. She chose regular Earl Gray, a cup of which was priced as high as a kids' meal at a hamburger joint.

At least she had a view of the street, Tara reflected, which meant she didn't have to watch everyone else eating. Besides, she reminded herself, she would indulge in a hearty peanut butter sandwich when she got home.

The heavy outer door whispered open and a man paused there, surveying the interior. Chance. If he expected to join her, Tara was going to give him a good tongue lashing. A quiet one, of course, in view of their surroundings.

But he sat halfway across the room, at a small table beneath a reproduction of a Renoir painting. Giving Tara a brief nod, he examined the menu with a pained air.

She didn't suppose he minded the prices, so she wondered why he was concerned. It embarrassed her, that his frown deepened when the waiter set a pot of tea and a cup in front of her and went away. Darn it, the man was perceptive enough to realize she couldn't afford the food, but she didn't want his pity.

Tara spooned a couple of sugar cubes into her tea. That ought to give her enough energy to get through the interview. The aromatic scent was soothing, too, although the liquid was still too hot to drink.

Resting her chin on her palm, she gazed out the window. The first flush of rain had washed away a layer of accumulated dust, and the storefronts gleamed. Even the young people hurrying by looked well scrubbed.

The table shifted, as if something had been set on it. Glancing down, Tara caught her breath.

In front of her sat the giant cream puff, cherry and all. As she stared, a slice of carrot cake sailed in her direction from the dessert cart.

Tara caught it in midair, noticing the confused glances of other diners. She wondered how much they had seen.

Turning in her seat, she leveled a disapproving stare at Chance. Oblivious, he handed a credit card to the waiter and nodded in her direction.

It seemed tacky to put everything back. Tara's indecision turned to amusement as a saucer of flan floated to take its place beside the carrot cake.

This time she fixed Chance with another quelling look. He smiled with the mock innocence of a child caught with one hand in the cookie jar but on the verge of improvising a brilliant excuse.

Tara couldn't stop herself from lifting a fork and sampling the cream puff. Then, because people were watching, she assumed a blasé expression and tasted the flan, as well.

There wasn't much she could do to foil Chance's sport, not without creating a scene. Besides, it took all Tara's self-restraint to take dainty bites instead of stuffing herself.

She didn't know how he'd arranged these tricks. Since his father owned a special-effects business, he must have plenty of technology to draw on, although the way he'd stopped the puddle from splashing her was truly amazing.

Well, if she ever needed a magician for a party, she

might hire him. Other than that, she decided as she finished the flan and launched into the carrot cake, Mr. Chance Powers had gone to all this trouble for nothing.

Chapter Ten

Rather than move Harry back to his old school or to the one closest to Denise, Tara decided to give him another chance at the school near Chance's house. It was a bit of a drive, but he missed his friend, Al, and the other kids.

The principal didn't look happy to see Harry again that Monday, when his suspension ended. She gave a wistful glance out her window at the denuded bush, which was struggling to put forth a few feeble buds, then signed the papers to reinstate him.

However, Harry's teacher, Mrs. Reed, smiled through the open doorway when she saw him approaching the classroom, which reassured Tara. Except for the incident with the fork at his old school, and the latest hassle concerning the fire engine, her son had no history of behavioral problems.

"I promise I won't mess around anymore," Harry said as she double-checked his backpack to make sure it included his lunch. "But can't I see Chance once in a while?"

"Absolutely not." Tara flicked a graham cracker crumb from his cheek. No matter how careful she was to wash her son's face, food seemed to hide in the pores and reappear later.

The little boy sighed. "Okay." Then, spying someone over her shoulder, he called, "Hi, Sammi! I'm back!"

A ponytailed girl hurried up, brimming with the latest news about which child had been beaned by a softball and who had a new baby sister. She and Harry disappeared into the room.

Adjusting her purse strap on her shoulder, Tara returned to her car. The appointment at the accounting firm hadn't yielded any results, and she needed to photocopy more résumés today.

She hated looking for work. The worst part was the sense of futility as ad after ad and interview after interview led nowhere.

The rest of the day dragged. Tara checked with employment agencies and called the personnel departments of several large companies. She had to struggle to keep her tone brisk and professional, and to hide her growing anxiety.

At two-thirty she left to go collect her son. Normally, she would have arranged for afterschool care, but now she couldn't afford it.

Today, Tara discovered as she hunted for a parking space in the crowded lot, was Field Day, a special event at the school. The children took fitness tests and competed in a mock Olympics.

Also, according to a flyer she found crumpled on the ground, the children were applying mathematics to measuring their jumps, and being assigned to read about great sports figures. It seemed like a creative idea, and it obviously appealed to the parents, many of whom had come to watch.

As she joined the crowd observing through a chain-link fence around the athletic field, Tara spotted a heavy-set figure in a dark suit. Even from behind, the white blaze in his black hair identified him as Raymond Powers.

What was Chance's father doing here? She supposed it was natural to want to see his grandson, but she doubted Raymond had interrupted his day out of fond indulgence.

Chance had warned that his father might try to exploit Harry's supposed talents. She wished she could laugh off Raymond's interest, but no one with sense would take the man lightly.

Deluded he might be about this magic nonsense, but unlike Chance, he had no scruples about his conduct. Also unlike Chance, he might decide to use his money to fight her for custody. She would have to be careful that what she said gave him no grounds to declare her unfit.

"Mr. Powers?" She came up from behind and had the satisfaction of seeing him start. "What a surprise!"

He swung around, assuming a broad smile. "It's not every day I get to meet my grandchild."

"Harry doesn't know yet," she said.

He drew her away from the knot of parents so they could speak privately. "You haven't told him about his father and grandfather?"

"Chance wasn't around for most of his life," she said. "I thought the news might come as a shock. Also, I don't know yet what role your son can and will play. The last thing I want is for Harry to get attached to him and then be disappointed."

It was close enough to the truth, she thought. And it would sound reasonable in a court of law, a lot more reasonable than a declaration that a man who believed in sorcery wasn't fit to be around his son.

"He's quite a good little soccer player." Raymond indicated the field, where a game was in the final stages.

"They're playing kickball."

"Whatever." Steely eyes regarded her. "Despite my son's failings, I would like to provide for my grandchild. And get close to him. It must be difficult for you, working and raising the boy alone. I could make things a lot easier."

You mean bribe me to turn him over. Tara bit her lip. She had to gauge her words carefully.

"I've done all right so far," she said. "I really couldn't accept any help. It's my responsibility to provide for my son."

"You're making this difficult." From the way his hands balled into fists, Raymond Powers had grown tired of the verbal fencing.

"Making what difficult?" she asked.

"The boy has gifts." The man dropped his pretense of grandfatherly warmth. "Gifts that need to be developed. By keeping him from his father's family, you're denying him his birthright."

"What birthright would that be?" Tara challenged. "Are we talking about uprighting tipped wineglasses, or—what is it you wanted Chance to do in your business negotiations? Mind reading? Or was that mind control?"

"Nobody's proposing any such thing for Harry," Raymond huffed. "Not at this age, anyway."

"Mind control doesn't exist, at least not without drugs and torture," Tara snapped, grateful that the distant shouts of the players kept her words from reaching the other parents. "As for accepting your help, no responsible mother would let you anywhere near her child."

Fury washed across Raymond's face. "Your son is descended from a great family. I have no idea what abilities he has inherited, but if you possessed even a little imagination, you wouldn't dismiss our claims so easily. You have no right to deny me access to him. We'll see what a judge says about—''

As he spoke, he stepped forward, his body bristling with menace and one hand extended as if to shake her. Then, in midsentence, Raymond froze.

A disbelieving expression crossed his face as his hand stuck en route to gripping her arm, half flexed so that it formed a claw. His body leaned toward her at a threatening angle, but it was obvious he couldn't move.

Tara's first thought was that he'd suffered a stroke. Then, just beyond him, she saw Harry.

The boy stood braced, eyes narrowing as he glared at his grandfather. His mouth trembled, not with fear but with determination.

He blinked, and Raymond straightened, then froze again as Harry regained his concentration. Tara wanted to deny what she was seeing, but unless this were a pre-arranged charade, her son was controlling the older man.

Harry didn't look as if he were playing tricks. He looked very, very angry, and in his eyes she saw both the boy she knew and the man he would someday become.

He had flown to his mother's rescue. Doing so had revealed, to her and to Raymond, exactly how powerful her son could be.

"I'm all right," she said.

Harry let out a long breath. Raymond stepped back, stunned.

Other parents and children hurried past them. A few regarded Tara oddly, but with all the distractions, she didn't think anyone had grasped what was happening.

"You should tell him the truth," Raymond said.

"I can see that I'll have to." She watched him coldly until the man, after one last glance at Harry, strode away.

"Who was that?" asked Harry.

She couldn't say the words *your grandfather*. It would be too abrupt. "Chance's father."

"Chance doesn't like his father, does he?"

"Oh, he mentioned that, did he?" Tara slipped one arm around her son's shoulder. "So who won the game?"

"We did!" The boy gave a happy skip. "Al kicked the ball! Not real hard, but not too bad, either. And he did it all by himself."

This time, Tara understood what he meant. A lot of things made sense now: the fork turning in midair, the fireman believing the school was ablaze, even the water that splashed into an invisible barrier as she crossed the street in Westwood.

They made sense, but it alarmed her to think what kind of sense. She was going to have to consider this matter at length.

She was also going to have to find a way to tell Harry about his father. Raymond had left her no choice.

HIS ATTEMPT TO IMPRESS Tara with his magic last week had failed miserably, Chance reflected as he sat eating a pita sandwich made with leftover tabbouleh salad and hummus.

Rajeev no longer had time to cook. Staring through the kitchen window into the twilight, Chance could see why.

Across the courtyard stalked a matador, executing a paso doble with the dancer portraying his scarlet cape, who was of course his sister. The ritual of the performance turned them into figures from a life-and-death drama.

Chance wondered how he would have reacted while interviewing housekeepers if, instead of the pleasant, courteous young man who had presented himself, he had encountered this glowering figure covered with the dust of a Spanish corrida.

In the dance, Rajeev was as fierce as his alter ego was easygoing. Vareena, that feisty figure who brooked no arguments in real life, yielded with grace.

Why couldn't Tara yield a little, too? Not that Chance wanted to change her, but he wished he could find the key that would open her eyes to the truth.

"Master?" said the house, which had been reprogrammed.

"Yes?"

"O esteemed one, o revered figure—"

"Sarcasm?" said Chance. "From a computer?"

"I have analyzed the responses of the Tara person," said the tenor voice. "I like her attitude."

"If I wanted a house with attitude, I wouldn't have reprogrammed you," he said. "Let's go back to the way you used to be."

"I shall make adjustments," said the computer. "Perhaps your esteemed self would be interested to know that the Tara person is approaching the front door, according to my sensors."

Chance bolted from his seat. "Well, let her in!"

"Does she know today's password is 'cockroaches'?"

The doorbell rang. "Never mind," he called as he hurried down the hall. "I'll let her in myself."

As he opened the door, Chance registered the fact that Tara was alone. He also noticed how uneasy she looked, as if it had taken all her courage to approach him.

"Please come in." He held the door wide.

"Raymond knows about his grandson and he wasted

no time trying to get his hands on him.'' She didn't budge from the front step. "I told Harry the truth about you today. He's anxious to move back in, and I'm willing to consider it, on one condition."

It took a moment to absorb so much information. Chance's joy at seeing her and learning that he might soon have his family back was mitigated by the news about his father.

He should have expected as much from Raymond. The man's first thought on learning he had a grandson had apparently been not paternal but predatory.

"What condition?" He didn't care; he just wanted her and Harry to come home. But obviously she cared, very much.

"No magic," she said.

"No magic?"

"The only thing you will teach my son is how *not* to control other people," she said. "And you can't do that hocus-pocus stuff yourself, either. Not so much as a salt shaker flying from one end of the table to the other. You know as well as I do that Harry will follow your example."

She didn't understand what was involved, Chance thought. "We need to discuss this. It isn't a simple matter. Please come in."

As she hesitated, he feared for a moment that she might leave. Then she followed him across the living room and through the courtyard, where Rajeev and Vareena, in the throes of their practice, ignored them. Chance had to pull Tara out of the way at one point or she might have been trampled.

"They certainly take this seriously," she observed as the two of them entered the office.

"A bit too seriously, I'm afraid." Not in the mood to sit, Chance leaned against his desk.

"I hope they win a trophy or they'll be devastated." She folded herself onto the couch with a hint of coltishness that he found endearing. Tara's light brown hair had acquired russet highlights, no doubt courtesy of her hairdresser girlfriend, but the frank olive eyes and expressive mouth were so familiar, they made him ache.

"I hope they don't forget to have fun." He indicated his wet bar. "Would you like something?"

"Got any cream-puff pastry or carrot cake?" she asked. "They were delicious, by the way. Thank you."

"My pleasure," he said. "Would you settle for cream soda?" At her nod, he filled two glasses with ice and poured the soft drinks, glad to have something to do.

"Raymond showed up at school this afternoon," she said. "I won't go into detail, but your father made a threatening movement toward me and Harry froze him. It was like that game children play, where they turn into statues, but this was real."

"Your son is amazing." He handed her a glass. "I mean, our son."

Slipping off her shoes, Tara curled on the couch. The instinctive action revealed, to Chance, how much she had come to think of this place as home, and he felt himself warming. "I've been struggling with these concepts all afternoon. Magic can't possibly exist, yet I saw it."

"It's rare," he conceded.

"I don't see how this is possible." Tara clinked her ice cubes moodily. "If people have such powers, why aren't they better known? Why haven't they been studied and evaluated?"

"Because very few people have them." Chance sought

the right words to explain. "In the past, those who displayed them openly were executed as witches."

"You're saying people hide it out of fear?"

"I'm saying very few people survived to pass on their inheritance." He hoped she was ready to learn the rest of what he knew, but he had to broach it cautiously. "Most of the time, the abilities people possess are limited and unreliable."

"Why is your family different?" She clutched her glass as if hanging on to the only solid thing in the room.

He wished he could gather her into his arms and reassure her. But Tara didn't need comforting words. She needed the facts.

"Some of my ancestors purposely married their own relatives to strengthen the powers," he said. "My father and mother were cousins. Distant ones, but both had—have—some abilities."

She stared into space before speaking. "Is that why you wondered whether your mother regretted having you?"

He let out a long breath. "Yes. She didn't realize either how talented I would be, or how Raymond would seek to exploit me. Fortunately, I seem to have inherited her ethics."

"And Harry's like you?" she asked.

"Harry has much more potential than I ever did."

"How can that be?"

This was the tricky part. "Even though you don't have magic talents, there's a psychic link between us that may have influenced him. I think it has to do with our past lives."

She groaned. "Now I've got to start believing in that, too? Chance, I don't like this. I want us to put it aside and live like normal people."

"I'll do whatever it takes to get you back." Realizing from her start of alarm that she was thinking of that intimate night in the tower, Chance added, "I mean, you and Harry. Of course, you'd live in your own suite, just as before."

"Then you're willing to teach him how *not* to use these abilities?"

"If I can," he said. "These aren't parlor tricks, Tara. Our son's urges are going to intensify as he gets older. With adolescence, they may explode."

"But you'll teach him restraint?" she pressed. "And set the right example by not doing this stuff yourself?"

Although he confined his magic to minor conveniences, Chance wasn't looking forward to giving them up. "You mean the next time somebody lets the air out of your tires, I'll have to call a tow truck?"

She stared at him. "You did that yourself?"

He shrugged. "But I won't, if you don't want me to."

"I don't."

"All right," he said. "When can you move in?"

"Tomorrow. I'll bring most of our things while Harry's in school."

"Consider yourself rehired," he said. "Although you don't have to work if you'd prefer not to."

"Of course I'll work!" Setting aside the glass, she stood up. "Don't bother showing me out. I know the way."

As she opened the door to the courtyard, passionate Spanish music wafted in. A matador and his cape swirled past, stalking the moment of truth.

Still uncharacteristically submissive, Vareena let her brother fling her about. In a way, Chance mused, he'd gotten his earlier wish for Tara to yield, as well.

He only hoped the terms she'd set wouldn't prove impossible to meet.

HARRY BOUNCED on the car seat beside Tara as they wound through the canyon. Ever since she'd told him that Chance was his father, he'd been happier than if it were Christmas and his birthday rolled into one.

"I won't do any more tricks, I promise!" he said. "Unless someone's trying to hurt you. Then it's okay, isn't it?"

"Nobody's going to hurt me," she said. "I told you, Raymond Powers wouldn't have done anything."

"I guess not," mumbled her son, unconvinced. "Hey, there's that funny mailbox."

"I noticed." Today, Tara was surprised how easily she followed the route. The landmarks jumped out at her, making each turn unavoidable. She didn't think she could have gotten lost if she'd tried.

As they pulled into the driveway, she tried to recall the password Chance had given her earlier. He'd moved on, through some quirk of humor, to insects. Oh, yes, today it was dragonflies.

Having brought their luggage earlier, Tara had only a few personal items to carry this time. It was fortunate she didn't expect any help from her son, because the moment they stopped, he leapt out and began running around the grove, shouting hello to the trees.

Watching him, she felt a tug at her heart. Harry belonged here. He loved Chance, and the feeling was clearly mutual.

She wished she had a better idea how she felt about the man. Since seeing Chance again yesterday, Tara had been trying to avoid thinking about the feelings that he stirred, but she couldn't any longer.

Whenever she came near him, they were drawn toward each other instinctively. It was difficult to walk without brushing against him, and hard to look at his face without staring into his eyes.

Being together was like finding another part of herself. Beneath the surface lay a longing to merge as they had that night when they made love.

Since she'd learned the truth about Chance's identity, the events of that Halloween had gradually seeped from the recesses of her brain into conscious memory. With growing clarity, Tara recalled the inevitability of their retreat into the tower and how she had experienced his sensations along with her own.

There was no rational explanation for it, yet she had encountered the same phenomenon whenever she and Chance met, beginning with the job interview. It was his self-control that locked her out most of the time, for which she ought to be grateful.

But she didn't feel grateful. She felt frustrated. Never in her life had Tara wanted anything as much as she wanted to regain that closeness with Chance.

If she expected him to honor their agreement, though, she had to resist her impulses. A deal was a deal.

Finally Harry rejoined her and they mounted the porch. "Dragonflies," she said.

The door swung open. "I've been thinking about ships," said the house. "I'm not too keen on being called the *Queen Mary,* but how about *Nautilus?* Or *Calypso?*"

"Don't forget the *Titanic,*" Tara couldn't resist answering. "Or the *Lusitania.*"

"Ah," said the house. "I've missed you."

She had missed it, too.

Chapter Eleven

"Towels?"

"Check."

"Sunscreen?"

"Right here."

"Beach ball, toy shovel, bucket?"

"I got 'em, Mom."

Tara finished crossing items off her list. "I guess we're ready to go, then."

Chance resembled a beast of burden as he led the way into the garage. There was no possibility of jamming the cooler, the beach chairs and the umbrella into the sports car, so everything got lashed atop the Lexus.

"You'd think we were migrating to a foreign land instead of going to the beach for the day," Tara muttered as she got into the passenger seat.

Harry hopped in back, fidgeting as he fastened his seat belt. "I'm going to dig a hole to China! And make the ball fly way up high and hang there! Boy, is everybody going to stare!"

Tara turned to face him. "You're going to do what?"

His little face grew solemn. "Nothing, Mom. But it would be neat, wouldn't it?"

Chance swung into the driver's seat. "Everything's lashed down. Let's hope we don't hit a strong wind."

His smile warmed Tara. This past week had gone so smoothly that it was hard to believe she'd ever been away. As for Harry, he'd skipped about the house in a state of near ecstasy.

It had been with a sense of relief that Tara resumed her work on the computer. Although she was still getting used to Chance's programs, she enjoyed the financial field and found it challenging.

And nothing beat having a job, except maybe having a family. But she had that, too, in a way.

She and Chance had agreed to act as much like a normal family as possible, for Harry's sake. That was why, on this Saturday morning, they'd decided to take advantage of the spring weather and visit the beach.

Tara had taken Harry on picnics before, but with just the two of them it hadn't felt as festive as today. Leaning back, she thought of the sandwiches she'd packed, along with sodas and cupcakes. Fixing food for a man made the occasion more special.

She was also looking forward to reading and working on her tan while Chance batted balls and assisted in the construction of a sand castle. Having a parenting partner was a definite plus.

"What if we see somebody drowning?" Harry asked from behind her. "Can't we use magic to rescue them?"

"Only if the lifeguards can't," responded his father as they approached the freeway. "And they're pretty darn good."

"What if some bad guys with guns start to shoot everybody and—"

"Harry! That's enough." Tara knew better than to get sucked into playing the what-if game. Her son had been pelting her with such questions since he learned how to talk. What if he didn't like his preschool teacher? What if he forgot his lunch? What if the rain fell up and chocolate candy was good for you?

It was, she supposed, an attempt to feel in control of his world by rearranging the rules. Well, the world had a way of asserting itself, and sometimes mothers had to do the same thing.

"Do you know how to swim?" Chance asked.

"I took lessons but I'm not very good," Harry admitted.

"If the surf's calm, I'll teach you. I used to swim competitively in college."

Tara could picture him as a swimmer. He had the right kind of body—lean and hard, the muscles firm but not bulky. Maybe that came from cross-training; she'd noticed that Chance went for jogs in the morning, as well as working out on exercise equipment in the spare bedroom of his suite.

A sideways glance showed her the casual power of his frame, highlighted by a red T-shirt and red, white and blue swim trunks. The man exuded confidence as he steered up an on-ramp, head tilted, gray eyes hooded in the sunlight.

She wished she remembered more of how he had felt in her arms that Halloween night. Instead, she had a jumbled impression of intense longing and fiery fulfillment. What Tara missed were the specifics: the roughness of his skin, his herbal scent, the pressure of his mouth against hers.

Thinking about it brought back the sensations in a rush. Most of all, she remembered being inside his mind and seeing herself through his eyes.

With a jolt, she found herself staring from another perspective, higher and to the left, at the freeway unrolling before them. She felt a masculine tightness at the core, and a twist of yearning that strained her self-control.

Not my self-control. His.

With a flicker of scarlet, the light glinting off a passing windshield turned to fire. For one stunned moment Tara saw herself surrounded by a circle of flames, and then cold blasted against her skin, bringing her back.

Chance adjusted the air-conditioning vent. "You looked hot."

Blinking off her daze, Tara said, "I had the oddest image, as if I were trapped in a fire. I must have been dozing."

"Or experiencing a far memory." Chance glanced back to make sure Harry wasn't listening. "From a past life."

Tara wanted to reject the explanation, but how could she? The sensation had come as she was merging into Chance's consciousness, the way she'd done that night in the tower.

A far memory. Past lives. *Gobbledegook.* She pictured Denise making circles around her temples and uttering spacy "woo-woo" noises.

The best course was not to worry about explanations. Surely as long as she and Chance kept their distance from each other, whatever dangerous passions lay slumbering would remain there.

There was no better cure for dark thoughts than a trip to the beach, Tara reflected as they exited the freeway. Rolling down her window, she inhaled the zest of salt air and heard the mewing of gulls.

Funky cottage-style buildings pressed close, their signs advertising bikinis, in-line skates and surfing gear. In the back seat, Harry stopped playing a hand-held video game and began bouncing.

"I haven't been to the beach in years," Chance admitted as he watched for a parking lot. "What shall we do first, Harry?"

"Dig!" said the little boy. "No, swim! But let's toss the ball before that."

Regret skewed Chance's smile. "I wish I could have watched him at every stage. I'll bet he's been a delight."

"You could have helped change diapers, too," teased Tara.

"Diapers? My son?" he murmured. "I'm sure he was *born* potty-trained."

"That sign says Beach Parking!" Harry announced. "See? I can read it!"

Beaming like the proud father he was, Chance angled into the lot, paid the attendant and wedged the car between a motor home and a van. "Let's hit the sand!"

What they hit instead was reality. It took at least ten minutes to unstrap the gear and drag it to an open space on the beach. Several times, Tara noticed Chance eyeing the equipment as if wishing he could waft it into place.

Once a strap nearly smacked him in the face, but stopped in midair. "Oops," he said, and let the thing whap his cheek. The sight of the red mark gave Tara a twinge of guilt, but she forced herself to remember that there were larger issues at stake.

With some help from her, Chance got the umbrella unfurled, the chairs set up and the cooler positioned. But spreading a blanket on the sand nearly proved his undoing.

His antagonist was a gusty breeze. Every time he flung out the blanket, a mischievous zephyr would catch the corner and pile it into a heap. When Tara grasped the far end, the center of the blanket wrapped around itself as if trying to form a figure eight.

"Is it always this hard?" Chance wiped a film of sweat from his forehead. "I've taken it for granted that the thing would lie down when I told it to."

"I seem to recall battling quite a few blankets in my time," she admitted.

"I guess I'm spoiled." Laying the cover on the ground, he began tugging it into shape.

"Dad!" Harry loved using the nickname although he still seemed shy about it. "Let's play ball!"

Giving up on the spread, Chance shrugged off his shirt and ran to join his son. The green-and-white ball flew between them.

After an application of sunscreen, Tara stretched out on the lumpy blanket, propping her head on a cushion. She could feel her skin cells browning one degree at a time, and the tension easing from her body.

Occasionally, using her hand as shade, she would check on her son. It was an old habit, and now, even though she trusted Chance to supervise him, she couldn't help monitoring his activities.

After a while, Harry became impatient and whacked the ball wildly. It flew over Chance's head and, to Tara's dismay, flew toward a baby crawling on the sand.

With a lunge, Chance flung himself forward and smacked the ball away in the nick of time. Wrenching himself to avoid falling atop the child, he landed heavily on one hip.

The baby clapped in delight. Buried in a magazine, its mother remained oblivious.

While Harry raced after the ball, Chance rubbed his side. It would have been a lot easier to use magic, and Tara felt responsible for his soreness.

"Need a rub?" she called.

With a pained smile, he shook his head. "Not in public, anyway!"

Did she detect some wishful thinking? "Don't push your luck!" she teased back.

He wouldn't, of course. He knew as well as she did that they had to keep their distance. Not that Tara quite believed Aunt Cynda's story about them stirring up old dangers, but she *had* seen those flames on the freeway.

Hauling out plastic shovels and buckets, father and son settled onto the sand near her. Under Chance's direction, they began constructing a castle.

Harry ran happily back and forth fetching water to shape the sand, while his father laid the foundations of an impressive structure. Other children wandered over to watch and soon joined in the work.

Great walls took shape, along with turrets and battlements. At least, Tara thought that that's what they were called.

From a beach bag, Chance produced small plastic banners and planted them in the towers. But the castle wasn't finished. While Harry bragged to the other kids that "That's my dad!" Chance set to work digging a moat, with a piece of driftwood for a bridge.

Retrieving her camera, Tara framed several shots. The best part was the radiance on Harry's face and the slightly embarrassed pride revealed in every gesture Chance made.

As she put the camera away, she recalled that, all these years she had imagined Harry's father as an enemy who might try to take her child. Instead, he was enriching the boy's life.

"No!" she heard Harry shout. By the time Tara could

scramble around to look, a large black dog was bounding through the castle, leaving a ruined mess.

A scowling older man whistled to the dog. From his hand dangled the leash that, according to posted rules, should have been attached to the dog's collar. The man didn't even bother to apologize.

The sand of the fallen castle shifted and stirred into mounds as Harry glared at it. Chance caught his arm. "No," he murmured. A plume that had almost become a tower fell back in a heap.

Down the beach, the irresponsible dog owner let out a yelp and clutched his bare foot. Tara caught a couple of curse words and wondered what he had stepped on.

She chose not to notice the way her son hummed to himself, his misery vanquished. Visitors had littered the beach with odd bits of junk, from plastic cutlery to twist-off bottle caps. There was no reason to ascribe the man's misfortune to anything but bad luck.

"Time for a swim." Chance raised an eyebrow at his son. "Ready to practice?"

"Beat you to the water!" Harry scampered off.

Tara sat in one of the chairs to watch. Although the ocean looked calm today, she never underestimated its wildness, and wanted to keep an eye on her son.

Riptides and sudden drop-offs in the sandy floor could pose unseen hazards, although she knew Chance was a strong swimmer. Also, this early in the season, the closest lifeguard tower had been left unmanned.

Tara hated to admit it, but she felt grateful for the knowledge that, in an emergency, Chance could use his sorcery. Even that must have its limitations, though.

Then she forgot her worries as she watched father and son cavort in the waves. After they tired of their im-

promptu swim lesson, Chance swept Harry up and swung
him around.

The man's torso gleamed like beaten copper in the
sunlight. The breeze ruffled his thick black hair, empha-
sizing the contrast to Harry's lighter coloring.

Chance lifted the boy onto his shoulders. Laughing,
Harry reached for the sky, and Tara's heart swelled.

She wanted to be part of this moment. Abandoning the
blanket, she raced toward the water.

HE WATCHED HER come, her slim body alive with enthusiasm. Try as he might, he couldn't escape a heated image of those long limbs tangling with his.

As he swiveled about, giving his son a ride, Chance
could feel Tara's approach. He tingled with awareness in
a dozen unexpected places.

It troubled him that she could be so much a part of his
life, and yet reject an essential element of who he was.
Worse, they would never again be able to experience that
unique blending of the physical and spiritual unless he
were certain they could both handle the consequences.

"Faster! Faster!" cried Harry, and Chance whirled
around. He had to be careful; with the sand shifting underfoot, he could easily lose his balance. This time, he
couldn't use a tweak of magic to right himself.

Until today, he hadn't realized how much he depended
on his magic as a backup. It had given him the boldness
to take risks that might otherwise have proved daunting.

How much of what Chance Powers had become was
due to this confidence? Maybe he owed more than he
suspected to his secret abilities, even though he had refrained from applying them to business.

Today's experiences had also helped him understand
the frustrations of others when they couldn't even make

a blanket do their bidding. And although the beach ball wouldn't really have harmed the baby, for the first time he could imagine how it must feel to see danger and be powerless to stop it.

As for the dog owner stepping on a sharp object, Chance had a suspicion his son had arranged it. Well, he couldn't blame the boy, but it would be important for Harry to grow beyond seeking revenge.

When Tara reached them, she slipped one arm around his waist without thinking. The contact sent a quiver of delight up his spine until, startled, she moved away.

"Come spin around with us!" called Harry, shifting his weight on Chance's shoulders.

"Not me! I'd get dizzy." She braced herself to resist the pull of the surf.

Beneath the calmness of the day, the ocean maintained its steady roar, loud enough that they had to shout to be heard. But it wasn't necessary to talk. Just being together was enough.

Chance swung his son down, and they moved farther out in the water to practice diving under the waves. Losing the fear of water while maintaining a healthy respect for it was vital for proficiency at swimming.

Beside them, Tara cut through the surf with natural grace. In the water, she lost any trace of awkwardness, moving with the sinuousness of a seal.

Whenever Chance glanced away from Harry, his gaze was drawn to Tara. He would catch the glint of her smile, or the flick of her gently rounded rump as she dived, or a tantalizing hint of breast as she curved onto her back.

Then his attention returned to his son. The day's activities must be catching up with the boy, who paddled with short, tired strokes.

"Time for lunch." Chance boosted Harry out of a large wave and turned him toward shore.

"You're doing great," Tara told her son. "You've got a real feel for the water."

He gave a grimace that was half appreciation and half dismissal. "Can I do a few tricks on the beach, Mom? Like put our sand castle back together?"

When she shook her head, he pouted until she reminded him that they'd brought sandwiches and chips, with chocolate cupcakes for dessert.

"Cool!" He headed for shore with renewed energy.

The boy wouldn't always be so easy to control, Chance reflected. He wondered if Tara had given any thought to what would happen when Harry hit adolescence.

His powers would multiply at the same time that he was experiencing a natural drive toward independence. By suppressing him so rigidly now, she risked inciting him to rebel later.

Surely, in time, Tara would soften her stance. Chance would do his best to persuade her, but until then, he intended to abide by their agreement.

A shriek from near the surf line grabbed his attention. Turning, he spotted a young woman treading water, her screams nearly swallowed by the ocean's roar.

Farther out, a young man, evidently her companion, struggled as a strong current yanked him along a course parallel to shore. From the sediment-filled swirl of the water, Chance judged it to be a riptide.

These churning currents were common along the coast. Experienced local swimmers knew enough to let themselves be carried along, gradually working their way to the edge of the riptide and then out of it.

But this couple, judging from their pallor, were tourists. The woman appeared safely outside the current, but the man was wasting his energy struggling to break out at a ninety-degree angle. Judging by the way he thrashed about, he would soon exhaust what was left of his strength.

"Get Harry out of the water!" Chance ordered, and Tara hurried to comply. With his son headed for safety, he focused on trying to reach the swimmer's mind.

He summoned an image of peace, of smoothness, of easing toward the edge of the current. But the man's panic blocked him. The man was too far-gone to benefit from mind control.

On shore, people ran in the direction of a distant life-guard tower, but the riptide was swiftly yanking its victim away from shore. By the time help could arrive, it might be too late.

Cutting through the water, Chance headed toward the distressed swimmer, but even as he swam, he could see it was useless. The flow carried the man away from him much too swiftly.

The man went under, bobbed to the surface, flailed around and sank again. There was no time to waste.

Holding himself a safe distance from the roiling river within the sea, Chance pitted his mind against the ocean, trying to calm the current for even a moment. His consciousness filled with a darkness that pulsed with immense power against which his skills were useless. It did not yield, not even slightly.

Grimly, he turned his attention back from the sea to its victim. There was only one course left. It threatened to reveal his use of wizardry in front of dozens of onlookers, but Chance could see no other choice.

Beneath the swimmer, he visualized a clear hard surface. Straining in concentration, he raised it to the surface of the waves. Tricks with umbrellas and splashing puddles had never required this degree of concentration.

Chance felt unsuspected reserves of strength pushing to the fore, lifting and easing the surface until it floated free of the riptide. A lifeguard, halfway to the victim, stared in disbelief.

The man lay suspended atop the waves, unnaturally straight as if sprawled on an invisible platform. Slowly Chance dissolved the support.

The man coughed and sputtered as he folded into the waves, but, clear of the current, was able to stay afloat. Catching him from behind, the lifeguard towed him landward.

Turning toward shore, Chance saw people standing along the beach staring at the water with varying degrees of confusion and amazement. He'd never done anything so dramatic before, certainly not in public.

It had violated his agreement with Tara, as well. But he knew she wouldn't have wanted him to let the man drown.

No one noticed when he emerged from the water, except the woman and boy who came running to meet him. Everyone else was watching, far down the shore, as the lifeguard helped the swimmer onto the sand.

"You were great, Dad!" Harry skipped back and forth along the waterline. "Wow!"

"Are you all right?" Tara took his arm, and Chance was surprised to find himself drained. He leaned against her until they reached the blanket, where he sank down.

"I could use some lunch," he said.

Tara wore a thoughtful expression as she set out the sandwiches, chips and soda. By the time she and Chance were ready to eat, Harry had already wolfed down his meal along with a cupcake.

Two of the children who had helped build the castle were taking turns burying each other in the sand nearby. Harry ran to join them, brimming with enthusiasm.

"He doesn't seem to realize that man nearly died," Tara said.

"I hoped you would approve, even though I did break my promise." Chance felt his strength returning as he finished one sandwich and reached for another.

"Of course!" Tara pushed back a hank of hair. "That was miraculous."

"I suppose it was." He thought of the little girl he had saved from being run over, long ago. "That's not the first time I've been able to preserve a life. I tend to forget what a special gift this is."

She nibbled at her cucumber and cream cheese sandwich. "Do you think Harry could learn to do that?"

"That and more."

Her gaze turned to her son, now half-buried in sand, his face smudged with peanut butter. He didn't look like a miracle worker.

Tara plucked a slice of cucumber from her sandwich and studied it as if it held the secret of life. "Seeds."

"What?"

"There are seeds here. Maybe we should save them and plant them."

"Are you speaking metaphorically or literally?" he asked.

"What?" Her startled glance met his. "Oh, metaphorically, I guess. I mean, when we plant a seed, we never know exactly what will grow, do we?"

"Like with kids?"

"Yes, I suppose. We think that they'll be like us, but sometimes they aren't. Then how much should we try to

steer them, and how much do they have a right to choose
their own direction?''

Chance didn't answer. He could tell that Tara needed
time to reconcile her conflicting impulses.

Finally she ate the cucumber slice. ''There are plenty
of seeds at the store. But there aren't any other boys like
Harry. All right, Chance. You can train him. But only for
emergencies like this. No more making people step on
sharp objects, even if they deserve it.''

''I'll do my best.''

He knew the day would come when, regardless of his
parents' wishes, Harry would insist on spreading his
wings. But that day, he hoped, was still far away.

Chapter Twelve

Tara was transferring data from Chance's business calendar onto his personal calendar for the month of June when she saw the conflict.

"Uh-oh," she said, which was probably not the most professional response but the first thing that came to mind.

"What?" Looking up from his computer, he wore the glazed expression that comes over men's faces, and sometimes women's, when they've been hovering in cyberspace too long.

Sitting at the auxiliary desk he'd installed for her in the home office, Tara grimaced at the calendars. "Would you believe the Powers Financial Corporation's annual dinner is the same night as the dance competition?"

"The one Rajeev and Vareena have been practicing for all this time?" Chance shook his head. "What a shame."

There could be no question of shifting the date of the dinner. The hotel ballroom had been reserved months ago, and printed invitations had gone out last week.

Not only staff members and their spouses but many clients would be attending. Chance was planning an elaborate event that would be a combination annual report, pep rally and big blast.

Nibbling at her pencil eraser, Tara tried to figure out a way around the dilemma. "Harry could still go, but I'd hate to miss being there to cheer them on."

"My staff and clients are pretty straitlaced," Chance said. "If experience serves, they'll bail out by eleven. Any chance the dancers will still be at it?"

"I'll check with Rajeev."

As it turned out, the winners in the dance competition wouldn't be announced until midnight. The event was scheduled for the Green Friars Country Club, a typical Southern California hybrid that rented meeting rooms to the public while maintaining a private golf course.

"It's about a fifteen-minute drive from the hotel," Tara told Chance after filling him in on the timing. "With luck, we can at least get there for the finale."

He tapped some information into the computer and logged off. "Sounds good. Now, if you don't mind, we've got a two o'clock appointment we're almost late for."

Tara hadn't seen anything on his calendar for today. "Did this come up suddenly?"

"No." A hint of mischief quirked at Chance's lips, then vanished so quickly, Tara wasn't sure she'd interpreted correctly. "It's more of a surprise."

Her first impression was that he planned something of a personal nature, but that seemed unlikely. In the weeks since she and Harry had returned to the yet-unnamed house, she still hadn't learned to read Chance's moods. Perhaps she never would.

She could tell that he enjoyed his occasional practice sessions with Harry, which left the boy eager for more. And Chance always treated Tara with courtesy and charm.

But there'd been no more suggestions of nocturnal visits to his whirlpool bath, and no more trips to the beach, either. She knew he was acting wisely, but she missed the closeness.

"Are we going to see a client?" Tara asked as she fetched her purse.

"We're going to make some preparations for the annual dinner." He held the door for her.

Although the firm's public-relations director was in charge of the event, Tara knew Chance took a keen interest in everything from the items on the menu to the presentation itself, which had a theme of "Up, Up and Away."

Were they going to rent a hot-air balloon? Would he be buzzing the ballroom with model planes? Tara wouldn't put anything past her boss.

It seemed odd, though, when they parked on a side street near ritzy Rodeo Drive. Women in designer suits clicked by on high heels, carrying shopping bags emblazoned with the names of famous shops. What sort of dinner preparations could they possibly make here?

Chance hadn't spoken on the way. His gray eyes had an opaque cast, but his mouth kept curving with amusement.

In a business suit woven of subtle shades of blue, with a hand-screened silk tie, he radiated sophistication. It was hard to picture him as the powerful swimmer who had plunged through the surf.

Well, not that hard. Actually, Tara's imagination outdid itself when it came to picturing Chance in a state of undress.

The firmness of his hands on the car door as he opened it reminded her of the way he had stroked her that night in the tower. The swing of his lean hips, angling out of the low seat, brought back sensations so achingly sweet that Tara had to force her thoughts away.

The heat of the sun helped dispel her traitorous imagination, and she concentrated on the shop windows as they passed. She saw no prices displayed, and guessed the elegant handbags, shoes and ensembles cost more than she could hope to afford.

Tara took only a casual interest in fashion. She knew she was probably wearing last year's colors and the previous year's shoes. Even in her crisp business suit, it would be hard not to feel dowdy on Rodeo Drive, where pencil-thin ladies swirled along the sidewalk with the remote air of models on a runway.

For once, she was glad she'd inherited height and a lean frame, but she wished the Loveliness Fairy had zapped her with a bit more grace. It didn't help to realize that the leather on the backs of her heels showed multiple scrape marks.

"Whoa!" She was nearly past the small boutique when Chance caught her arm. "This is where we're going."

"Here?" There were no clothes in the window, only a bouquet of exotic flowers in a Chinese vase, set against a draped cloth. "Is it a florist's shop?"

"Not exactly. It's called Fleur's."

Tara recalled seeing the name in one of the magazines at Denise's salon. A former designer for a Paris couturier, the woman now custom-fitted her creations to a select clientele, by appointment only.

Tara wondered when Fleur had begun designing for men. She also wondered why Chance wanted her opinion of his new clothes, since he had such unerring taste.

Inside the shop, they found themselves in a plain waiting room. A receptionist asked their names and announced them through an intercom.

They had barely sat down when Fleur herself emerged. Strong-boned and graying, she introduced herself to Chance and Tara in a softly accented voice.

If she hadn't met Chance before, that meant he hadn't yet selected his clothes. Tara wondered how this aristocratic designer would react on learning her creations were to be evaluated by a woman in a discount-store suit and scraped heels.

Fleur led them to an inner room, more spacious and better lit than the waiting area. On a side table sat a silver coffee service and a selection of pastries.

"Not knowing mademoiselle's tastes, I made a few selections from my collection." The designer indicated a half dozen exquisite creations displayed on mannequins.

Even though she knew a mistake had been made, Tara couldn't help staring longingly at the array. In addition to a rainbow-hued formal gown with a high collar and plunging neckline, there were floating dresses and suits of varying lengths. She also noticed a clingy pantsuit styled like a tuxedo but made of an opalescent fabric so delicate, it might have been cut from a cloud.

"What do you think?" Chance asked in a low voice, his head tilted toward Tara.

"They're incredible," she said. "But these are women's clothes."

Fleur raised one eyebrow. "Indeed," she said. "That is what I design."

"But I thought—" Tara shifted her attention to Chance, and saw his suppressed amusement bloom into a grin. "We're shopping for me?"

"As my personal assistant, you need to be properly

attired at the dinner," he said. "Naturally, I will absorb the cost."

Objections flew in and out of Tara's brain like gnats at a picnic. She couldn't possibly accept. These clothes must cost a fortune. If anyone heard about this, they would jump to the wrong conclusion.

Of course, if people heard—which they surely would, sooner or later—that she was the mother of his child, they were going to jump to those conclusions anyway.

"Oh" was what came out, barely audible.

"If I may say so, mademoiselle has the perfect figure for fashion." Fleur lifted a soft, midcalf-length suit with a scarf-collared jacket from the display and held it close to Tara. The fabric had pink overtones glimmering with hints of blue and yellow. "This is very flattering. Also, I would suggest trying the tuxedo. These are the new colors for the season. A veritable rainbow, *n'est-ce pas?*"

Tara wished she could spot a price tag so she would know exactly how much Chance was going to be set back by all this. Then she realized that the idea of a price tag had probably never entered Fleur's mind.

"I suppose I could try them on," she said.

Chance made himself at home on the couch close to the refreshments. "That sounds like a plan."

The dressing room turned out to be almost as large as the salon. A seamstress and Fleur assisted Tara, removing her garments with practiced ease and fitting her into the calf-length suit.

It was a bit large, but a few swift tucks by the seamstress made it fit. Tara nearly asked whether alterations were included in the price, then bit her lip. This wasn't the kind of establishment where such things mattered.

She knew Chance put great emphasis on image for his business, but was he really willing to pay—how much?

A thousand dollars? More likely ten times that, Tara reflected with a gulp.

Maybe he could return the outfit for partial credit after the dinner. But she doubted it.

As Fleur added a perky hat that provided an air of casual sophistication, Tara realized the woman reflected in a trio of mirrors would do Powers Financial Corporation proud.

She had high cheekbones and fine skin, with a touch of haughtiness offset by her wide eyes. It wasn't really Tara, but some alternate version whom even Fleur regarded with admiration.

On the other hand, she couldn't stop thinking of the other uses to which that money could be put. Ten thousand dollars was enough for a down payment on a condominium. It would make a great start on a college fund for Harry. Or she could back Denise in opening her own salon.

But it wasn't Tara's money, it was Chance's. He had already promised to set up a trust fund for Harry, and as for those other things...well, they weren't going to make his business look good at the annual dinner.

Swallowing hard, she complied with Fleur's suggestion that she model the outfit. Holding her head high and hoping her pink cheeks didn't reveal too much of her inner conflict, Tara strode out of the dressing room.

Chance was setting his coffee cup down when he spotted her. He seemed, for a moment, to stop breathing.

Then his gaze traveled from her jaunty hat down the flowing lines of the suit, touching her shoulders, breasts, hips and legs before returning to her face. Blinking a couple of times as if caught off guard, he gave a small nod of approval.

But did he really like it? Tara didn't know what his

reaction meant. She felt his intensity in every snap of her nerve endings, but maybe she was misled by her own prickly awareness of the man.

She wished, this once, that she could be inside his mind the way she had been when they first met, experiencing his thoughts instead of guessing at them. He was deliberately blocking her, of course, she told herself as she made a turn around the room. That was for the best, to keep each other at arm's length.

If only they hadn't met the way they did, and then come back together with so many issues between them. The pure masculine appreciation shining from his face was something Tara wanted to relish. She wanted them to be simply a man and a woman.

But what good would that do? They couldn't allow themselves to fall in love, she told herself as she retreated to the dressing room. She wasn't convinced it would be dangerous in the way Aunt Cynda believed, but it would certainly threaten her peace of mind.

Never again did she want to make herself vulnerable to a man's disapproval the way she had been to her father's. Her self-reliance had been won at a high cost. As she changed into the cloud-colored tuxedo, Tara wondered if she would ever trust a man enough to marry him.

She cherished every moment she spent with Chance. But the distance he resolutely kept between them was her margin of safety. For different reasons, neither of them dared cross it, and that, she decided, was for the best.

Yet when she stepped into the salon again, and saw the tenderness with which he watched her, she felt less certain. Depths of emotion turned his eyes to silver, and the amusement on his face had been replaced, for one unguarded moment, by yearning.

"Which do you prefer?" she asked.

"They're both amazing." His voice had a hoarse note.

"The tuxedo is more businesslike," she said.

Fleur chuckled. Until that moment, Tara had almost forgotten her presence. "How differently people react! One of my customers is purchasing that suit for her wedding."

"For a bride?" Tara regarded herself in the oversize mirror and realized the slim lines and pale, iridescent material would make an offbeat but charming picture at the altar. "What a clever idea!"

"Is the groom wearing a black gown?" Chance teased.

"He's Scottish," said the designer. "I believe he's wearing the traditional kilt."

"That settles it," Tara said. "I'm wearing the skirt and jacket. No way am I going to the annual dinner as a bride!"

"I have to admit, I did like that outfit better," Chance admitted. "Or if you prefer one of the dresses—"

Tara sensed that Fleur had instinctively chosen the two creations that best suited her. "No, we've made the right choice."

The seamstress took additional measurements in the dressing room, and Fleur promised to have the suit delivered within a week. "And the hat, as well?"

"Why not?" Tara said.

"And may I suggest some shoes..."

By the time they were finished, the suit and hat had been augmented by slippers and an evening bag. Tara refused to let herself think about the cost.

She emerged onto the street feeling giddy. "Thank you," she told Chance as he guided her back to the car. "That was very generous."

"Pure selfishness," he assured her. "I'm the one who

gets the pleasure of looking at you. Now we'd better hurry. We just have time to pick up Harry.''

Usually Rajeev handled that responsibility. "Why? Are we going somewhere?''

"Well, it *is* Friday." Chance unlocked the car and held the door for her. "And we have been invited to a special event.''

Today seemed to be Chance's day for surprises. Tara doubted he could top their visit to Fleur's, but she was willing to play along.

CHANCE KNEW he was driving the sports car a shade too fast on the way to pick up Harry, but he needed to take the edge off. He'd been stretched thin ever since he saw Tara in those sensuous clothes.

The impulse to buy her a fabulous outfit had seemed innocuous at the time. But the air between them had been charged from the moment they entered the salon.

This past week had turned into a mixture of joy and agony. Being close to Tara and yet unable to touch her had left Chance with energy so tightly bottled, he feared he might explode.

At least he'd had the distraction of helping Harry explore his gifts. Practicing mind control to prevent squirrels from running into the street had amused them both, and saved at least one creature's life.

It was too bad there existed no aptitude test for wizardry. Chance suspected his son would score off the top of the chart. Fortunately the boy had been raised with a strong sense of values.

Now, in front of the school, Harry waited beside a thin boy wearing glasses, whom Chance recognized as his friend, Al. They were grinning and joking with other children.

Harry's eyes brightened at the sight of the sports car, and he ran over. Tara barely had a chance to lean her seat forward as he scrambled pell-mell into the back.

"Can we go by the video store and see if there are any new games?" he demanded. "Can we stop at the book-store and see if they have the new *Goosebumps?*"

"I've got a better idea," said Chance. "How about going to a carnival?"

"A carnival?" Tara asked.

"My old school is a few miles away," he explained. "It's a private school, and this is the annual fund-raiser. It occurred to me we could swing by there and maybe catch a ride on the Ferris wheel."

"It occurred to you?" said the car. Since undergoing a tune-up and oil change the previous week, it had quit nagging, but now it apparently felt free to inject its whiny voice into the conversation. "Excuse me, but didn't you program the directions into my map two days ago?"

"I wish Al and Sammi could hear this!" Harry leaned over the seat back. "I bet they've never been in a talking car!"

"And with luck they never will be, either." Chance switched off the computer's voice. "The reason I wanted to drop by is that my great-aunt Cynda has volunteered to staff the fortune-telling booth. I thought it would be fun to see her in action. Besides, she's dying to meet Harry."

"The fortune-telling booth? I thought she didn't have much success at seeing the future," Tara observed.

"She doesn't. That's what makes her perfect for a school fair," Chance pointed out. "She can tell people what they want to hear, and they'll go away happy."

"But it isn't honest," said Harry.

"Everybody knows fortune-telling isn't real." Tara

stopped with her mouth ajar. "I mean—things like that *usually* aren't real. And even Chance can't foresee the future, can you?"

"Thank goodness, no."

"I think it would be neat!" cried Harry.

Both his parents reacted at the same time.

"You haven't—" began Tara.

"Don't tell me you've started to—" said Chance.

They exchanged glances. "You can't see the future, can you?" Tara finished for them both.

"Me?" said their son. "I wish I knew what was going to be on the math test next week! But I don't."

The school, tucked away on a quiet street, looked much as Chance recalled it. Stucco buildings dating to the 1920s sprawled across a tree-shaded campus, which, this afternoon, had turned into a riot of color and motion.

In addition to the Ferris wheel, he spotted a roller coaster and half a dozen other high-speed rides, along with a carousel and a small railroad that wound its way about the grounds.

Booths sold food and souvenirs, while one tented section was set aside for games. Shooting galleries and ring tosses never seemed to lose their appeal, even in the age of computers.

As Harry led the way, skipping onto the grounds, Chance wondered if he should consider transferring his son here. Not only Chance, but his cousin Lois and several other relatives had attended West Oak Academy.

He decided a decision could wait, perhaps until junior high. After all, the boy had made friends and begun putting down roots at his current location.

It would be useless to try to temper Harry's high spirits until they'd sampled a few rides, so for the next hour the three of them flew, bounced, zoomed and shrieked their way around the grounds.

Finally, after downing pizza and corn on the cob, they headed toward the booth area. Signs advertised an astrologer, a palm reader and Madame Lucynda and her crystal ball.

"Does she really have a crystal ball?" demanded Harry.

"Well, yes." Tara had worn a faintly amused expression since they arrived. To Chance's surprise, she hadn't even objected to riding on the roller coaster. "At least, it's a ball, and it appears to be made of glass, so I suppose it qualifies."

"How does it work?" the boy pressed.

"That all depends on Cynda," Chance said.

"It's a way to help her focus?" In their practice sessions, his son had quickly grasped the usefulness of specific exercises and objects as an aid to concentration. "I get it."

A teenage couple emerged from the blue-and-gray-striped tent as they approached. "She's terrific!" the boy said. "She told us we were meant for each other!" The kids walked off beaming, arm in arm.

Chance felt a twinge of envy for such uncomplicated happiness. But then, he had nothing to complain about, he reflected as he slipped one arm around his son's shoulders and, taking Tara's elbow, guided her inside.

Red light from a scarlet-shaded lamp gave a cheesy air of mystery to the interior, where the crystal ball sat atop a paisley-covered card table. Behind it perched Aunt Cynda, forming an exotic picture with her sharp black eyes, long Gypsy dress and oversize turban.

"Wow!" said Harry.

"Impressive," murmured Chance.

"Oh, bosh," said his great-aunt. "I look like a refugee from Halloween. Lois found this getup at a costume shop. You'd think a woman who works for a special-effects company could do better than this, wouldn't you?"

"It's a pleasure to see you again," said Tara.

"And you, too, of course." The woman fixed her gaze on Harry. "This little urchin would be your son, I take it? Fine young fellow. I think I'll take him back to my cottage in the woods and fatten him up, shall I?"

"That's from *Hansel and Gretel!*" Harry didn't look in the least intimidated. "That's make-believe! Can't you do anything real?"

"I'm sure Aunt Cynda tells very good fortunes," reproved his mother.

"Did you buy tickets?" asked the lady, adjusting her turban. "It's for a good cause, you know. The library needs new computers. I remember when children read books, don't you? Now it's all CD-ROM and bits and bytes and the Internet."

"I like to read," said Harry. "But I like the Internet, too."

"That's the gift of youth," said his great-great-aunt. "To put complex truths in a nutshell. Well, boy? Step up and let us see what the future holds."

Tara peeled a ticket from her roll and handed it over. As Harry plopped into a chair and stared at the crystal ball, Chance noticed Tara stiffening.

He wasn't aware of letting down the guard between them, but he sensed her thoughts. What if tragedy lay ahead? What if they learned something they didn't want to know?

Aunt Cynda had never seen anything accurate yet, but it didn't seem polite to say so in front of her. Besides, she *had* figured out their past lives as Valdemar and Ardath.

Maybe that was why Chance, too, felt a tremor of apprehension as his great-aunt began to speak.

Chapter Thirteen

"You like baseball," said the fortune-teller.

As Harry nodded, Tara nearly laughed at her own misgivings. It was a safe bet that any six-going-on-seven-year-old boy would fit that statement.

"And squirrels," Cynda added.

Tara's amusement evaporated. She remembered her son chattering about keeping a squirrel from running in front of a truck, and wondered if anyone had mentioned the incident to Cynda.

"An important event will occur soon." The older woman frowned into the glass, which had turned from clear to milky. Tara wondered what had made it do that.

"My birthday!" said Harry. "It's in July."

"No. Sooner." Cynda tapped the ball. "It's on the fritz again, darn it. Ah, there we go. I see people dancing. Do you like to dance?"

"No, but Rajeev and Vareena do," said the boy.

Behind them, Tara heard someone slip into the tent. Glancing back, she glimpsed a short young woman with glossy dark hair, chic pearl earrings and a suit trimmed in braid. Before she could ask what Lois was doing here, Tara noticed a name tag that said Organizing Committee Chairwoman.

"Rajeev and Vareena?"

"They've got this dance competition the same night as Chance's company dinner," Harry said. "You really saw them?"

"More or less," murmured Cynda.

"Who's going to win?" he asked.

"Excuse me?" The older woman peered at him dubiously.

"Are Rajeev and Vareena going to win the trophy?" Harry persisted.

Cynda's forehead puckered. "I don't see any trophy. Just smoke."

"Maybe you've got a short circuit." Releasing Tara's arm, Chance looked around for a plug.

"It's not electrical." The fortune-teller drew herself up. "It's merely tired from a long day's work. And so am I."

"I came to suggest you take a break," explained Lois. "You've been here three hours, and we're open until eleven. You ought to take a walk and eat some dinner, Gram."

Standing, the fortune-teller yawned and stretched. As she came around the table, Tara could see trouser cuffs peeping from beneath the black robe.

"If you don't mind, I'll take my little nephew with me so we can get to know each other. You young people can reminisce about your favorite teachers and that one everybody hated—what was his name? The economics teacher." Without waiting for an answer, Cynda took Harry's hand and out they walked, discussing what to purchase for dessert.

Tara wasn't used to letting her son wander off with other people, but, she reminded herself, Aunt Cynda was a relative. So was Lois, she mused as she greeted the younger woman.

The three of them strolled out of the tent together. "How's the carnival going?" Tara asked.

"Even better than we expected!" Lois waved to a passing couple. "We've set a goal of raising ten thousand dollars, but I think we'll surpass that. And of course we'll be open tomorrow, as well."

"This must have been a lot of work," Chance said. "I'm surprised you found the time."

"Oh, I've always wanted to give something back to my school." Lois sounded sincere, and Tara realized it was unfair to assume the young woman was always calculating her own advantage. She might work for Raymond and even admire him, but that didn't make her his clone. "Please tell Denise I've had lots of compliments on my hair. That lotion really works!"

"She'll be glad to hear it."

They reached the midway, which was growing more crowded by the minute. Over the music of the carousel, Chance asked, "How's Dad's acquisition going, of the software gaming company? Everything under control?"

"'Under control'?" repeated Lois. "Now, there's a phrase Ray would appreciate! Every time we meet with their board, they bring up a new demand. We're setting up a session to see if we can iron out our differences."

"Good luck," Chance said, and nearly collided with Cynda and Harry, who were consuming huge snow cones.

"Gram! That's not a very healthy dinner," Lois scolded.

"It's my appetizer," said Cynda, deadpan.

Harry grinned, displaying a face smeared with snow-cone coloring. In the shifting lights, it might have been either red or green.

Lois smiled. "You two make a charming pair. A couple of scamps!"

The five of them joined company as Lois made sure her grandmother followed the snow cone with a sandwich. Banter flew, and Harry and his older cousin seemed to hit it off.

"Maybe she's finally developing a maternal instinct," Cynda observed after her granddaughter excused herself to see to her duties. "Let's hope she eases up on her ambitions. Not that I'm a keep-'em-in-the-kitchen type, but there's more to life than making money."

Tara agreed. She'd enjoyed tonight's merriment and the comforting sense of being with family. She knew Harry had, too.

As for Chance, he was smiling as he guided them toward the car. Maybe, she thought, they'd finally hit on a comfortable balance that they could maintain, working and playing together without the risk of deeper involvement.

If she ached to put her arms around him, and if sensuous memories of their Halloween encounter still tormented her sometimes, that was an issue she could learn to deal with.

BY THE NIGHT of the annual dinner, Chance felt more like an orchestra conductor than a businessman. Although he had paid scrupulous attention to his clients' affairs these past weeks, he had also spent long hours making sure every part of tonight's presentation would hit the right note and rise to a crescendo of goodwill.

Thank goodness for the assistance of his staff, and for Tara, who proved invaluable when the work threatened to overload him. Hundreds of details had been arranged, surprises planned and a multimedia presentation honed to pulse-pounding entertainment.

In a way, the heavy work schedule had proved a blessing. It enabled him to keep his attraction to Tara pushed to the back of his mind.

Chance's only regret was that he hadn't spent enough time with Harry. Now that school had ended for the summer, the boy was chafing to use his magic, and a few hours a week failed to satisfy him. Once tonight was past, Chance vowed as he adjusted his cummerbund in front of the mirror, he would make time every day for his son.

"Excuse me," said the house. "Isn't anyone eating at home tonight? The fridge is full of leftovers."

Chance was so startled, he nearly dropped the slim wallet he was tucking into one pocket. "Did somebody call you or are you speaking on your own these days?"

"It's my duty to point out that some of the food is likely to spoil," sniffed the computer from an all-but-invisible speaker in the wall. "Really, couldn't you address me as something other than 'you'? I know I haven't yet chosen a name, but it seems demeaning."

Chance had more important things to do this evening than pacify his house, but he couldn't resist. "Abode?" he suggested. "Dwelling unit? Maybe I could call you by our address."

"Too impersonal," said the house.

"I'll give it some thought," said Chance. "Later."

After one more check in the mirror, he strode from the room. Behind him, the lights turned themselves off with a sigh.

Rajeev and Vareena had left for the competition an hour ago with Harry in tow. Chance had gotten so used to them twirling around that the courtyard lay strangely empty without them.

A smog-enhanced sunset filled the sky with a rosy glow. Chance hesitated in midstride, forming an image of that long-ago Halloween when he'd stood in the tower, peering down at the costumed guests.

That night, he'd been trying to figure out what direction to take with his life. He'd realized he couldn't stay with his father's firm and follow Raymond's wishes, but he'd been apprehensive about striking out on his own.

His mood had been far from festive. Noting that the revelers below were mostly casual acquaintances attracted by his flyers, he'd nearly decided not to bother making an appearance.

He hadn't so much glimpsed Tara's presence as sensed it. Struggling to reconstruct the experience, Chance decided it had been like catching a whiff of fragrance. He closed his eyes, wanting to retain these memories to treasure later, no matter what might come.

Now that the intense work of the past weeks was finished, he doubted he and Tara could continue as they were. The undercurrent between them grew more powerful every day. Yet he hadn't forgotten Aunt Cynda's warning about their union awakening danger.

For once, the Magician had no tricks, the Warlock no spells, the Wizard no wisdom that could protect them. Fate had woven an unseen tapestry, and Chance was as caught up in it as Valdemar had been in his long-ago quest to free his true love from a tyrant.

I just wish I knew who the enemy was. I hope it isn't some part of myself.

"Oh, you're out here!" Tara emerged from the far wing of the house. The rainbow hues of her suit blended into the sunset-tinged light, making her appear almost translucent. "We're going to have to hurry."

They'd planned to arrive well in advance, but a glance at his watch showed Chance he would barely beat his guests to the scene. "Let's go, then," he said, and offered his arm.

HARRY KNEW A COUPLE of the other kids; he'd met them while watching Rajeev and Vareena's dance classes. They were sitting on the floor in front of the folding chairs.

He plopped down between an African-American girl with long braids, and a boy whose frizzy blond hair made him look as if he'd stuck his finger in a light socket.

"My mom and dad made the semifinals," said the little girl, whose name was Marika. "How about yours?"

There'd been a preliminary competition the previous weekend at the dance school. Rajeev had told him something about it, although Harry hadn't paid much attention. "Yeah, they're competing tonight, too."

"Standard or Latin?" asked the little boy. Harry thought his name was Dag or Tag.

He didn't know, so he said, "Both." The other kids looked impressed.

From what Vareena had told him in the car, Harry gathered that this wasn't exactly the Olympics of ballroom dancing. It was more like a high school game between a couple of schools.

But the row of shining trophies sitting on a table at the end of the ballroom looked big-time to him. And grown-ups were filling the chairs around the dance floor, their voices abuzz with excitement.

The room was as big as a school gym, with banners stuck on the walls and clusters of balloons floating near the ceiling. Harry wondered whether the kids got to take the balloons home afterward.

He shifted, trying to get comfortable. The floor was made of wood instead of linoleum or tile. Probably that was because the Green Friars Country Club used to be a private mansion. From the outside, it resembled the Haunted House at Disneyland.

Harry hoped he could talk Chance into coming here with him sometime to explore. A big old house like this ought to have secret rooms and maybe even a treasure.

Static rumbled over the sound system, followed by a man's voice. "One, two, three, testing."

He saw the man and a woman, both in fancy clothes, standing at a microphone behind the trophy table. "Welcome to the second annual Kick Up Your Heels competition for beginning and intermediate dancers!" said the man.

"We want to build enthusiasm in the students from both our schools, and prepare them for competitions to come!" added the woman.

"The main point is to have fun!" said the man, and began talking about the semifinals and then the finals that would be held that evening.

When he finished, music blared and a bunch of dancers came galloping into the room. The guys had on tight pants and glittery jackets; the women wore floaty dresses with flounces and spangles, and one had pink feathers. Harry figured they must have been plucked from parrots, because what other kind of birds were that color?

The women were spinning and jumping, and the men stamped their feet the way Rajeev did when he was pretending to be a matador. Some of the ladies got tossed into the air and one rode around upside down on her partner's shoulders.

Harry got a not-so-happy feeling. Rajeev and Vareena were clapping and making little twirls, but some of these other people didn't look like beginners to him. They were really good.

For the first time, it occurred to him that his friends might not win. It didn't seem fair, not when they'd practiced so hard.

Maybe they needed a little help.

SET TO ROCK MUSIC and animated via computer, the year's investment highlights made a great show. While images danced on an array of screens and Chance's voice boomed over the music, the guests finished dessert and applauded lustily.

It was after eight o'clock and the dinner had gone perfectly. Everyone raved about the food—"Shrimp and salmon! Thank goodness it's not chicken like every other banquet!"—and the decor proved equally popular, with sections of the room decorated to suggest the gondolas of hot-air balloons.

Generally, Chance didn't believe in superstitions. But things were going a little *too* well.

As **he** acknowledged the applause, he wondered how Harry was getting along at the dance competition. The boy had enjoyed watching Rajeev's classes, but this might prove a long evening. He was glad he and Tara would be arriving later.

Tara. It took Chance's full concentration not to keep staring at her. The flowing suit with its delicate shadings brought out her innate grace. Tonight she was so radiant, he suspected she could light up the room all by herself.

But with the applause fading, he needed to collect his thoughts and resume his duties as master of ceremonies. "Now we've got a diversion for you folks," he said into the microphone. "In keeping with our theme of Up, Up and Away, and my reputation as a wizard of Wall Street, we've got a pair of uniquely talented entertainers. They're jugglers, they're magicians, they're comedians. Ladies and gentlemen, may I present Lee and Lew!"

As he spoke, two men ran out, juggling what appeared to be hand grenades and wearing suitably horrified expressions. The audience greeted them with cheers and laughter.

For the next ten minutes, the guests chuckled at similar antics. Then Lee and Lew announced that they needed a woman assistant, and settled instantly on Tara. The fact that she was standing nearby and was—in Chance's opinion—the most beautiful woman in the room might have had something to do with it.

She hesitated only a trace before stepping forward. Her delicate features wore a studied smile, and he could see she was fighting her natural shyness.

First, the pair pretended to saw her in half, with lots of stumbling and bumbling that would have filled Chance with alarm if it hadn't been so funny. Her hat ended up in one corner and her tousled hair reasserted its spiky independence, but in the end, Tara escaped in one piece.

Then they asked her to pick guests whose minds they would read. The "thoughts" relayed by the comedians were risqué without being offensive.

"Now that fellow over there." Lee pointed at Chance. "He's supposed to be a wizard, so he ought to be able to read your mind, eh?"

Tara brushed back a lock of hair, which promptly flopped forward again. "Well, yes."

"Lew is going over there to blindfold him. Then we're going to show you an image, and you have to try to transmit it."

It should be easy to play along with whatever gag the pair had in mind, Chance told himself as Lew tied a bandanna around his eyes. He'd had lots of practice blocking out Tara's thoughts.

What an irony, that they intended the whole thing as a joke, and yet had picked the one couple in the room who actually could read each others' minds. If, of course, he allowed it.

"Here you go!" said Lee, and Chance heard a shuffling noise that might have been a poster being lifted into view.

He hadn't intended to peek, but he found himself overwhelmed by curiosity. Surely it couldn't hurt to find out why the crowd was laughing, as long as he didn't reveal that he knew. After a moment's hesitation, he relaxed the barrier that he habitually raised whenever he felt close to Tara.

An image came to mind with unexpected sharpness, as if he were looking directly at it. It was a cartoon bull chasing a man up a profit-and-loss chart. The man, who bore a strong resemblance to Chance, clutched his rear end as he ran.

He could feel Tara's enjoyment of the humor. She was releasing the tension of the past few days, now that the evening had gone well.

Being inside her mind felt natural, and increasingly intimate. As the thought came to him, Chance knew it reached her, too. He was grateful for the distraction when Lee asked, "Are you getting anything over there?"

"Not really." But before he realized what he was doing, Chance rubbed one of his hips as if it was sore. The audience howled.

"Very good!" announced Lee. "Tighten his blindfold, will you?"

The cloth strained as Lew resecured the knot.

"Now try this one," came the voice from the podium.

Instantly, a picture formed in his mind, viewed directly through Tara's eyes from where she stood near the poster. He also caught a hint of her perfume, just enough to stir his masculine hunger.

This cartoon depicted a bear walking a tightrope, holding a balancing pole that looked like Chance turned sideways.

"Well?" said Lee. "See any stock prices falling in a bear market?"

"I'm getting an image of snow," said Chance. "It isn't a polar bear, is it?"

People applauded. When Lew removed the bandanna, Chance caught a trace of curiosity on the entertainer's face.

"Those two sure know how to communicate," said Lee. "And no, folks, that wasn't rehearsed!"

The pair finished by juggling shrunken heads that issued intermittent blasts of fire. "This is how Chance feels whenever the Federal Reserve Board announces a change in interest rates!" Lee cracked to the audience, and the comedians finished to thunderous approval.

With relief, Chance turned the program over to the band and invited his guests to dance, have another drink or help themselves to an extra dessert at a special buffet. He didn't think he could take much more public scrutiny while his mind was in a whirl.

The moment he let his guard down, the connection with Tara had been instantaneous, as if they'd practiced at length. It was stronger and clearer than before, as if something had been growing between them at the subconscious level.

Was that merely an extension of their natural attraction

and comradeship? Or did it mean the ties from a past life were reasserting themselves, regardless of anything Chance or Tara intended?

RAJEEV AND VAREENA DID turn out to be entered in both standard and Latin categories. Harry decided to wait and see how things went in the first round before he tried using his magic.

The standard semifinals came first. Twelve couples had to spin around the dance floor at the same time.

The announcer called out two kinds of waltzes—regular and Viennese—and something boring called the fox-trot, which didn't have anything to do with foxes. Harry thought at first his favorite would be the tango, which involved a lot of stamping and twitching.

But when the announcer called the quickstep and the pairs went galloping around the floor like a stampede of horses, he decided he liked this dance best. There were even a couple of collisions, at which the kids laughed uproariously.

"Cool!" said boy beside him, whose name turned out to be Dag.

A panel of judges made marks on score sheets as the couples whizzed by. Harry couldn't stop himself from listening in on their thoughts.

They liked the way Rajeev and Vareena did the tango, but they preferred a tall couple's fox-trot and, for the quickstep, a pair of dancers in scarlet costumes.

When the names of the six final couples were read off, Rajeev and Vareena weren't among them.

Harry glared at the judges. He wished now that he'd done something, but at least the Latin section was still to come.

A few minutes later, when the twelve Latin semifinalists were introduced, out came Rajeev and Vareena in different costumes, sleeker and tighter. This time they seemed even more energized, as if throwing everything they had into winning.

There was a blond couple who hadn't been in the other competition, as well as a chubby redhead teamed with a bald man. There was an African-American couple, too, who must be Marika's parents.

As the pairs took turns bowing to the audience, Harry wondered what he should do to help his friends. He didn't want any of the others to get hurt, just to stumble or run into each other. That ought to do it.

Then another thought occurred to him. "Dag," he said. "Which ones are your folks?"

The little boy indicated the blond couple. Okay, Harry would have to spare them.

"That's my parents." Marika pointed at the red-haired woman and the bald man.

She must be mixed-up. "No." Harry pointed at the African-American pair. "*Those* are your parents."

The little girl shook her head, chuckling. "No, silly! I'm adopted!"

Well, he couldn't zap the redhead, then. And Harry couldn't bring himself to trip the African-American couple, either, just in case Marika was playing a joke on him.

Then he noticed the other boys and girls sitting around the room, some in chairs, some on the floor. Did they all have parents out there?

Harry's heart sank. He couldn't go through with it, not even to help Rajeev and Vareena. Everybody here must have practiced long and hard, and they all had friends who were rooting for them.

As the competition began, the snappy music improved

his spirits. With passion and fire, the couples stalked and clicked through the cha-cha, the samba, the rumba, the paso doble and something called jive that looked like rock 'n' roll.

At least he could tell that the judges liked Rajeev and Vareena. They made the right kind of movements for the Latin numbers. Even without reading minds, Harry could see that the pair were well matched in height and style.

So it wasn't a surprise when the names of the finalists were read off, with Rajeev and Vareena's among them. Marika's and Dag's parents made it, too.

Harry let out a long breath. He was glad his friends were still in the running. He was glad he hadn't tried to help them, either. Now that he thought about it, he could see that it would have been cheating.

Among those applauding loudest was a dark-haired woman sitting across the room, behind a tall man. When the man leaned aside to talk to somebody, Harry got a clear look at her.

Boy, was he surprised to see Cousin Lois. Who would have thought she would take such an interest in ballroom dancing?

Chapter Fourteen

Tara had half a mind to give Chance the cold shoulder for the rest of the evening. He'd had no business popping into her mind, even if they were playing a mind-reading game.

Not only had he poked into her perceptions, she'd been unwittingly thrust into his. She didn't want to feel the way his heart speeded up when he looked at her. She didn't want to acknowledge the masculine heat that stirred when he inhaled her perfume.

The man was impressive enough when viewed from the outside. Even in a conservative tuxedo, there was no disguising his muscular build or the confident stance that bordered on arrogance.

Tara wasn't sure what to do with the warmth he aroused in her, but she did know that she couldn't act on it. In the last few weeks, she felt as if unresolved bits and pieces of her life had begun to fall together, but the puzzle remained unsolved.

She didn't know why she felt so strongly linked to Chance. She didn't know why she sensed danger whenever they grew too close. She only knew that the prospect of merging with him again threatened her self-control and in some way her very existence.

With the presentation finished, clients and staff members were gravitating to him. Chance recognized each of them with a tilt of the head and a subtle narrowing of his gray eyes, as if acknowledging a unique bond between him and that person.

Standing at his side, trying to view him objectively, Tara decided that part of the man's success came from the fact that he did indeed regard each co-worker and client as special. He never took them for granted or lumped them together.

This was part of Chance's gift, the way his intuition blended seamlessly with knowledge and experience. There was nothing magical about it, she supposed, but the results were amazing.

These reflections softened her uneasiness. When the others drifted away and Chance asked her for a waltz, Tara agreed.

Stepping onto the dance floor, she was reminded of the competition under way a short distance from there. She and Chance would never execute a waltz with the smoothness and elegance of Rajeev and Vareena, but that wasn't the point.

Tonight's dancing was not a performance but a combination of relaxation and, she supposed, communication. It was one way that men and women could reach out to each other without words—and without getting too deeply involved, either.

As the music soared, Chance led her firmly on a private trajectory. They were matched well enough in height, yet he dominated the space through which they moved, his powerful shoulders and straight back declaring a zone of privacy.

No one else could feel the way their bodies connected across several inches of air while they wove a pattern among the dancers. No one could see the electricity tingling between them.

Tara became aware of Chance in every pore, as if the sensuous fabric of her suit conducted and enhanced his presence. Her breasts prickled at the nearness of his chest. Silver excitement ran through her core as his thigh brushed hers.

"That was quite a mind-reading performance tonight, wasn't it?" he murmured. "I wonder what people thought of it."

"They thought we planned it," she replied, grateful for the distraction.

He regarded her quizzically. "Did it feel different to you? As if the connections were clearer?"

"Connections?" Tara tried to keep her edginess from showing. "You sound as if you're referring to some new kind of fiber optics."

He ducked his head, acknowledging her point. "I didn't mean it that way. But something's growing between us whether we want it to or not."

A primal twist of fear caught Tara off guard. Why should she be alarmed? Annoyed, yes, or possibly displeased, but why did her hands go cold?

An image flashed across the landscape of her mind so quickly that it was more of an impression than a memory. A wall of fire surrounded her and Chance as they huddled together against one wall of a high-ceilinged room. As she watched, a long, scarred wooden table burst into flames.

"Aunt Cynda's warning," she said, then realized the remark must seem to come out of the blue.

But not to Chance. Steering her around an older couple, he said, "You feel it, too? I'm concerned, but I don't see anything amiss."

The soft music segued into a rock number. Tucking her hand beneath his arm, Chance led her off the dance floor.

People gathered around as if they had been waiting to talk to him. Few had specific questions or concerns, Tara noticed. They were drawn by the man's magnetism and reassured by his strength.

She, on the other hand, felt far from reassured. Since the day she decided to return to his household, she had tried to persuade herself that the two of them could co-exist on a platonic level. The signs of their growing attachment had been everywhere but she had managed to ignore them, even that day at the dress shop when he had treated her with such tenderness.

Tonight she could no longer fool herself. He was right about the connection when their minds met. And the sensation of danger grew stronger by the minute.

She ought to leave as soon as possible. Not just this party, but his house and perhaps Los Angeles, as well. There could be no real safety, only the illusion of it, until she put as much distance between them as possible.

But I can't. The simple statement came from the heart, and frightened Tara more even than that half-imagined, half-remembered image of flames.

She didn't believe in fate, and yet from the moment she and Denise set out on their drive that long-ago Halloween night, some force had pulled her directly into Chance's arms. She didn't believe in unfinished business from past lives, either, but the night outside this hotel lay thick and waiting, like a panther stalking them.

With a wrench, Tara forced her attention onto a stocky man who was taking his leave of Chance.

"I've stayed too long," the man said with an apologetic smile. "I made them schedule the meeting late just to accommodate me, but I should have been there by now. I did tell them to start without me, but I'm chairman of the board, so they can't come to any agreements until I get there.''

Tara didn't know who the fellow was, but Chance obviously did. He knew all his clients. "I didn't realize—I mean, you're on so many boards, it hadn't struck me. The company is the one my father's trying to acquire, isn't it? I'm sorry, I didn't put two and two together until now. I keep strictly out of these matters, of course.''

"Oh, I know that." The man, whose name tag read Victor Moustaki, waved a hand in dismissal. "As a matter of fact, I started investing with you because your father recommended you so highly. I checked you out first, and he was right.''

"You're meeting with Ray tonight?" The timing set a red light flashing in Tara's brain. "Would you mind if I ask where?''

"The Green Friars Country Club," he said.

BEFORE THE FINALS in the standard competition began, a demonstration of show dancing by professionals had been scheduled. The grown-ups around him leaned forward eagerly, but Harry was tired of sitting on the hard floor and he'd seen enough dancing for a while.

He sneaked down an aisle and went to the dressing room to see Rajeev and Vareena. They were huddled side by side on a worn couch, while Rajeev anxiously inspected his sister's shoe.

"The heel is definitely loose," he pronounced as Harry entered. "There must be someone here who knows how to nail it down.''

"I am not dancing with a nail sticking into my foot!" protested Vareena.

"You should not get hysterical," said her brother. "We have come so far, what is a little pricking?"

"Maybe you could use Super Glue," Harry said from the doorway.

Rajeev looked up, his dark eyes approving. "An excellent suggestion. Do you have any?"

"Not on me," said Harry.

One of the African-American competitors spoke from a chair in front of a lighted mirror, where she was retouching her makeup. "The head of the judging panel usually comes prepared. I saw him heading for the coffee room."

"Thank you so much!" Rajeev jumped up. "Let us not waste time!"

"We should look after the boy." His sister got to her feet, keeping her weight off the troublesome shoe.

A slim hand came to rest on Harry's shoulder, and Lois spoke from behind him. "Hi, guys! Need any help?"

When the situation was explained, she volunteered to take Harry for a walk around the club. "It looks like a fascinating place, doesn't it? We should be back in plenty of time to see you compete."

"We would be most appreciative," said Vareena.

"The glue will need time to dry!" warned her brother. "We must find the judge at once!"

Lois drew Harry into the hallway to let the pair pass. "We'll be fine. Don't worry about a thing."

Harry wasn't sure Mom would want him wandering around the club with Lois. She'd told him very strictly to stay at the dance competition and not to go anywhere without Rajeev or Vareena.

But Lois was his cousin, the first one he'd ever met. They'd had fun together at the carnival, hadn't they? It probably hadn't occurred to Mom that she would show up here.

Harry knew better than to trust strangers. Not that he was afraid of them. Anybody who messed with him would get frozen in place, or see an illusion of policemen shooting at him. Unless the stranger turned out to be a sorcerer or—what was that other word that sounded so ferocious?—a warlock, like Dad.

But this was Lois, not some stranger. Besides, the dance demonstration was going to be boring until Rajeev and Vareena's turn came again.

"Where are we going?" he asked as they strolled down the hallway.

"Did you know there are some parts of this club that aren't open to the public?" Lois's eyes got big, like his teacher's did when she was reading the class a story.

"Like the kitchen?"

"That's one example." Opening an unmarked side door, she led the way up a narrow staircase. "Also the executive offices. And the locker room is for members only."

"Don't locker rooms smell funny?" Harry had been hoping to discover a game room.

"Okay, you convinced me. We'll skip the locker room!" Lois grinned, but she sounded more nervous than amused. They reached a landing, and through an open doorway Harry could see the second-floor corridor.

"What's here? Let's take a look." He started forward, but Lois caught his hand.

"These are the offices," she said. "It's only half of a second floor anyway, and it's not very interesting."

"Why is it only half of a second floor?"

"Some of the rooms downstairs have extrahigh ceilings, so they take up most of the second story. Come on, let's go see the attic!''

A squiggly feeling in his stomach troubled Harry. He thought maybe it was his conscience, or it might be the spicy leftovers Rajeev had fed him for dinner. "We should go back.''

Lois crouched down to Harry's level. She was a very pretty lady. "Actually, this is kind of a game we're playing. I need your help.''

"In the attic?'' he said.

"The man who built this house, a long time ago, modeled it after a castle somewhere,'' she told him solemnly. "There are secret passageways and hidden alcoves for spying on people.''

That sounded even better than a game room. "Who else is playing?''

"Ray,'' she said. "You know. Your grandfather.''

That was the man who'd been so mean to Mom on Field Day. "I don't like him.''

"You won't be anywhere near him,'' she promised. "In fact, we're going to snoop on him, sort of.''

Harry tried to think of what Mom or Dad would say, but he wasn't sure. He certainly didn't want to go sit on that hard floor downstairs while Lois had fun playing this game.

Dag and Marika would sure be envious when he got back and told them about his adventure! And Al and Sammi at school would be impressed, too.

"Let's just go have a look,'' said Lois.

They went up another flight of stairs. A sign said Off-Limits. Do Not Enter!

"Maybe it's not safe.'' The stairs *were* kind of creaky.

"They don't want the guests getting lost,'' Lois said. "Would I come up here if it were dangerous?''

"I guess not." Harry felt a bit better when she turned on the lights, although they were dim. Naked bulbs exposed a sprawling room with a peaked roof and sloped ceiling.

Along one side, metal folding chairs were stacked in rows. Built-in cabinets bore labels, most of which he couldn't read, but one said Table Linens, and another, Chandelier Bulbs.

He was trying to figure out how to pronounce the word *chandelier,* which was not on any of the first-grade spelling lists, when his cousin tugged him onward.

"Try to be quiet," she whispered. "Remember, this is a spy game."

There wasn't much else up here, just a lot of open space and dust. It was hard not to cough, but Harry did his best. He hoped the secret passageways weren't full of spiderwebs. In video games, you never had to worry about stuff like that.

"How do you know where everything is?" he asked.

"There was a lot of publicity when the house got sold and became a club, twenty years ago," she said in a low voice. "Ray clipped an article that gave the history and sketches of the floor plans. He had a feeling it might be useful. He's held meetings here before."

"Meetings?" said Harry.

They reached the far wall. Pulling a flashlight from her purse, Lois located a slim, vertical crack. She ran her hand up and down it, then pushed at several points. Just when she was starting to mutter some of those words Harry wasn't allowed to use, a panel slid open with a snick.

"Well, thank goodness," she said.

To his relief, Lois went through the opening first.

When he followed, Harry found they weren't in a narrow passageway but a small room.

When Lois turned off the flashlight, he saw a yellow pinprick shining in the wall. "It's a peephole," explained his cousin, steering him toward it. "Take a peek."

All Harry could see was darkness, with the point of light above his head. "It's too high." He stood on his tiptoes, but it wasn't enough.

"Here, let me help." Awkwardly, Lois boosted him up. She seemed shaky, and he guessed he must feel heavy. "Can you see now?"

He could, barely. He was looking down at a room with a long table in the middle. It was so far below, he felt like an angel floating in the clouds.

A couple of men in business suits were shaking hands and greeting each other. To his surprise, Harry discovered he could hear their words.

One man wondered where somebody named Victor was. Another guy complained that Raymond could have found a more suitable place to meet, even on short notice.

"How come I can hear them?" Harry whispered.

"It's the acoustics," said Lois, setting him down and rubbing her arm muscles.

"What's acoustics?"

"It makes you able to hear things. This room was designed so the owner could spy on people. It was in the 1920s and he was what they called a rumrunner. A gangster who smuggled alcohol instead of drugs. He must not have trusted the people who worked for him."

Harry didn't care about rumrunners. He wasn't sure what smuggling meant, and the only thing he knew about alcohol was that Mom used it to kill germs.

"I want to go back now," he said.

"Look! Your grandfather just came in!"

Harry knew enough about grown-ups to understand that Lois wasn't ready to leave. Anyway, maybe the game was starting.

When she lifted him again, he saw Raymond shake hands with the other men. Somebody asked about a device on Raymond's ear, and he said he'd just gotten a hearing aid, and wasn't it awful about getting old, but it didn't slow him down any.

Lois set Harry on his feet and took something from her purse. He heard a click, and she whispered, "We're here. Everything's A-OK."

His eyes adjusting to the darkness, Harry realized she was speaking into a little microphone. "How can he hear you?"

She clicked it off. "It's that thing on his ear. It's a receiver."

"Are we starting the game now?"

"In a minute." She squirmed uncomfortably. Harry wished there were somewhere to sit, but then they wouldn't be able to see through the hole.

"How does the game work?" he asked.

Lois stopped wiggling. "When we did it before, he just had me stand up here and listen while he was out of the room. This is better though. You can read their thoughts, can't you? I mean, you're such a smart boy, and Chance says you're awfully talented."

"Chance knows about it?"

"Oh, sure." Her voice sounded funny. It didn't take much of a mind reader to figure out that she was lying. "In fact, he asked me to work with you to help develop your abilities."

No, he didn't. If she'd been a stranger, Harry would have punched her for trying to trick him, but he knew better than to hit a lady. Besides, he might get lost trying to find his way back through that big dark attic.

"You and Ray are cheating, aren't you?" he said.

"What?"

"Listening to the men's thoughts is cheating." Harry was proud that he understood this.

Until tonight, he'd known that Chance and Mom disapproved of taking advantage of his talents, but it had seemed like just another grown-up rule. Kind of like no throwing balls in the house.

But it made sense now. He'd seen for himself how unfair it would be if he tripped the other kids' parents so Rajeev and Vareena could win.

"It's not cheating." Lois sounded as if she were trying to convince herself. "This is business. Everybody uses whatever angle they can find."

"What about Raymond?" Harry couldn't bring himself to call the man Grandpa. "Can he talk to us?"

"Only if he goes out of the room." Lois brushed back her hair, and he saw that she was wearing a device on her ear, too. "He won't need to talk to us if things go well. But if the other men won't cooperate, he might ask you to, well, give them a push. Do you know what I mean?"

"You mean make them do something they don't want to?"

"Just a little," she said. "Just until they sign their names."

A lump was forming in Harry's throat and he wished Rajeev and Vareena would come and find him. But how could they? Nobody would think to look in the attic, and they probably didn't even know he was missing.

He didn't want to use mind control on those men. It

wasn't fair, and he knew for sure that Mom and Dad wouldn't like it.

Maybe he could use mind control on Lois. Closing his eyes, Harry tried to make her take him downstairs. But her smell, flowery and soapy, mixed him up, and her rapid breathing made him nervous.

Trying to reach her mind felt like one time when a gnat had landed on his nose and he'd tried to make it come into focus. Other than crossing his eyes and getting a headache, Harry hadn't accomplished much. He wasn't having any luck with Lois, either.

Below, the men were sitting down when another man walked in. "Victor!" "Mr. Moustaki!" "We're certainly glad to see you!" They stood up and shook his hand.

"You fellows missed a great party!" said the newcomer. "They put on quite a magic show."

"Really?" Ray murmured, kind of squinting like he wasn't sure what the guy meant.

"Lee and Lew. They're jugglers, comedians, magicians, you name it. Hilarious." The man sat down. "Let's get started, shall we?"

"Anyone mind if I smoke?" When no one did, Ray lit a cigarette, then passed around some papers. "Gentlemen, I've drawn up a list of the issues we need to iron out...."

Lois shifted position and tried to wedge Harry onto her hip. He kind of felt sorry for her, but not very much.

This was much more boring than the dance competition, he decided as everybody below picked up the papers. They weren't jumping around or bumping into each other, and their clothes didn't even sparkle.

He decided to read his grandfather's mind. It would serve the old geezer right.

Peering through the pinhole, he fixed his gaze on Raymond. Immediately, he caught a sense of elation, but it had a dark undertone.

The guy felt sure he was going to triumph, but he had alternate plans—a whole tangly mess of schemes—if things didn't go his way. Trying to trick him would be like playing a computer game designed for grown-ups.

No matter how good Harry was, he realized, there would be rules he didn't understand. He might make his grandfather mess up a little, but not for long. Once Raymond realized the boy was tricking him, he would find a way around it. His brain was like a forest with paths that kept changing and hungry animals that hid in the trees and waited to drop on your shoulders.

Below, the man named Victor was talking. Pretty soon, Ray would expect Harry to read the man's mind, but he couldn't even understand what the guy was saying, let alone what he was thinking.

He didn't want to be here. It was such a strong feeling that Harry knew he had to do something. He had to beat his grandfather in a way that Raymond wouldn't expect.

It was the cigarette that gave him the idea. People shouldn't smoke; that's what Mrs. Reed had said at school. So he was going to do his grandfather a favor.

"Can you tell what—" Lois whispered.

"Shh!" Harry put all his energy into staring at Raymond. The man gave a twitch, as if he felt something, but he didn't seem suspicious. He started to bring the cigarette to his lips.

Harry gritted his teeth. Below, his grandfather's fingers tweaked and the cigarette landed right in Ray's lap.

It was hard not to laugh as his grandfather jumped up, furiously brushing his pants and cussing. The other men, who had been absorbed in their reading, glanced at him in confusion.

"What's going on?" Setting Harry on his feet, Lois put her eye to the pinhole. "Did you do something?"

"Raymond dropped his cigarette," he said.

She tried to pick him up again. "Well, come here. We're not finished."

"I'm tired of this." Dodging back, he could hear himself starting to whine.

Lois sighed. "Please help out, okay? If this fizzles, I'll never get promoted. Just read a few thoughts, would you? Something useful, and then I promise we'll leave."

He didn't believe her. After he read some thoughts, Raymond would want him to control somebody's mind. But Harry knew something they didn't.

A curl of smoke issuing from beneath the table told him the cigarette butt was still alive. Before long it would set off the smoke alarm or sprinkler system, or maybe catch Raymond's pants on fire.

Then they could all go home.

Chapter Fifteen

The uneasiness that had flowed around the edges of Tara's consciousness solidified into fear as Chance drove. Had the night been hung with red banners and flashing lights, it couldn't have raised any more alarms in her mind.

It couldn't be a coincidence that Raymond had scheduled a meeting for the same night and place as the dance competition. Lois must have overheard Harry telling Cynda about it, and passed the word along to her boss.

The question was, what was he planning and how did it involve Harry? Tara tried to reassure herself with the thought that Raymond had no reason to harm her son. Even if the boy refused to cooperate, what could his grandfather hope to gain by injuring him? But her deepest instincts told her this was exactly the situation Cynda had hoped to prevent.

Tara had tried phoning the club when they first left the hotel, but at this late hour, only an answering machine picked up. "He's just a little boy. I shouldn't have expected him to sit around by himself for hours. He's interested in watching the competition, but not *that* interested."

"There must be dozens of people there, maybe several

hundred," Chance pointed out. "Even while Rajeev and Vareena are occupied, Harry's not alone."

"A hundred people who aren't paying attention aren't worth one who is." Tara couldn't help blaming herself. "I should have anticipated this. I should have hired a baby-sitter."

"If you think some teenager could stop my father from getting what he wants, you underestimate Ray." Chance floored it through a yellow light. "But let's not torture ourselves. We're almost there."

He was right; there was no point in whipping themselves into a state of panic. Trying to change the subject, Tara said, "Those performers were terrific. You must have gone to a lot of trouble to find them."

"Every year, I try for a surprise. Powers Financial is known for putting on a good show." He whipped around a corner, then slowed as they entered a residential area. "That's why Victor was so eager to be there. Thank goodness he mentioned it."

"I hope people aren't offended that you left early." Tara had seen surprised expressions when Chance loped out the door, although he'd asked his staff members to explain that there was a family emergency.

"Frankly, I don't care." He tapped the brakes and turned, a shade too quickly, onto another street.

Faint sounds in the back of Tara's consciousness coalesced into sirens. She gripped Chance's arm. "Do you hear that? You don't suppose—"

"It might be anything," he said. "We have to stay calm."

Ahead of them loomed the Green Friars Country Club. Although she'd read about the place, Tara had never seen it before. With its three stories of Victorian gables and bay windows, it could have been transported from New England in the days of the Puritans.

Smoke whispered from an upstairs window, deathly pale against the night sky. Amid the jangling of alarm bells, people poured out the doors.

In that heart-stopping moment, Tara knew her worries hadn't been empty. "It's on fire!"

There was no place to park, so Chance pulled onto the sidewalk and killed the engine. "Let's go."

Jumping out, they clasped hands to keep from being separated as they raced into the crowd. People tried to wave them back, but they pressed forward.

It was fortunate that her height let her see over much of the throng, because she was the first to spot Rajeev. "Over there!" she cried.

In the clamor of approaching sirens, she wasn't sure Chance could hear, but he did. Plunging between the escaping guests was like swimming upstream, but at last they reached the housekeeper.

The anxiety in his eyes told Tara what she feared. "I could not find the boy," he said. "I have looked everywhere, but there is no sign of him or Miss Lois."

"Lois?" Chance asked.

"She said she would look after him," Vareena put in, shouting to make herself heard. "We thought he would be safer with her than by himself."

Tara knew Chance must be thinking the same thing. Lois had taken Harry somewhere else in the building, where he could spy on Raymond's meeting. But where?

"You stay here," he told her. "I'm going in."

"It is dangerous!" protested Rajeev. "I will go back myself."

"No!" Chance shook his head. "He's my son. And I might be able to locate him in ways you couldn't."

"I'm coming, too." Tara couldn't bear to wait here. Logic said she could accomplish nothing more than Chance could do alone, but a mother's instincts urged her to go to her child.

Catching her shoulders, he put his mouth close to her ear. "My life may depend on you being out here, so we can communicate. You can let me know instantly if Harry gets out on his own. And if I'm trapped or injured, you could guide the firemen to me."

"Take your cell phone, too."

He swore softly. "It's in the car. Besides, I've got a feeling—Tara, trust your instincts. That's our best hope."

Near the top of the building, a flame licked through a window. It seared a path directly across Tara's heart.

She wanted to rush in there in the blind belief that her love would lead her to Harry. But Chance was right. Their best hope was the psychic link between them. The connection they had been fighting against for so long was the thing they needed most.

"I think I understand," she said. "All right. I'll be here."

Fire trucks screamed into the parking lot, bristling with ladders. Several more halted along the street, followed closely by a paramedic unit and police cars.

"I'd better get in there before the firemen seal it off," Chance growled. He turned, and nearly collided with his father.

Perspiring heavily, Raymond struggled to catch his breath. "Have you seen them? Did they get out?"

"Lois and Harry? No." Chance's hands balled into fists. "Where are they? So help me, if they die because of you…"

"They were in the attic," Raymond gasped. "I never thought—the cigarette must have—I swear, that room went up so fast, the carpet must have been made of tinder.''

"The attic?'' Chance repeated, disbelieving. "Of all the insane, irresponsible places to take my son!''

"They were in a little chamber overlooking the meeting room.'' Raymond panted. "Come on. I'll show you.''

The two men ran into the house. They were barely in time. A police officer came by a moment later, securing the area.

"Is anyone inside? Does anybody know if people are missing?'' A fire official addressed the crowd through a megaphone.

Tara waved and shouted, but couldn't make herself heard. It was Rajeev who caught the man's attention and explained what had happened.

"The attic?'' The official gave an involuntary shake of his head. "That's the worst possible place. We'll get some people up there right away.''

As he departed, Tara forced herself to step away from the crowd onto a grassy median. Despite the adrenaline pounding through her arteries, she needed to concentrate.

Chance might be trying to reach her. And so might Harry.

THE FIRE HAD SPREAD really fast. Harry hadn't figured it would be any big deal, but before he knew it the whole room was filled with smoke and alarms were going off, and he could feel the heat even through the peephole.

Then Lois started acting crazy. "We're trapped! Get me out! Get me out!'' she screamed as if Harry were a grown-up who could take charge. The way she was panting like a cornered animal, he thought she might pass out any minute.

Mom had once shown him a videotape about fires, so

he knew that heat rises. They needed to get out of the attic right away.

Downstairs, the men were hurrying from the room. "Call Raymond!" Harry told his cousin. "Tell him to come up and get us!"

After a moment of blank staring, she produced the microphone and clicked it on. "Raymond? Raymond?" She tried for a while, but there was no answer. "It has a limited range. He must be too far away."

"Do we have to go all the way across the attic?" Harry asked. "Is there another way out?"

"I don't think so," Lois said. "I guess that's why this area was off-limits."

Part of Harry's brain told him to trust the adult and let her take charge. That was what six-year-olds usually did.

But it was Lois who'd gotten him into this mess. Although she wasn't shrieking anymore, he could tell she wasn't thinking clearly.

"You just do what Raymond tells you, don't you?" he said. "Well, he's not here now, so you do what I tell you."

To his amazement, she nodded. It made Harry feel good, until he realized that now everything was up to him.

THE LOBBY OF THE CLUB lay eerily empty, echoing with the shrill noise of alarm bells. Except for the scent of smoke, it looked quite ordinary, with its beige couches and worn carpeting.

Oversize photographs of the house's architectural details, from a weather vane in the shape of a unicorn to a distinctive gable, formed a display across the side wall. One room caught Chance's eye and sent his heart slamming into his throat.

It was a high-ceilinged conference room with a long table down the center. He had seen that room before, or one very much like it.

It was the room where Ardath and Valdemar met their deaths. *Curtains ablaze. Men shouting. Flames licking.*

He felt a shock of horror, and knew it belonged not only to him but to Tara. At this moment, she was seeing through his eyes, too.

"That's where you held the meeting?" he asked as they hurried past.

Raymond glanced at the picture in surprise. "As a matter of fact, yes." Chance shuddered, then forced himself to thrust the image from his mind.

He could still feel Tara with him, but the awareness faded as he moved farther from her. Their plan to stay in contact might not work, after all.

Firemen clattered into the lobby behind them as they sprinted past a main staircase. Rounding a corner in the heavy brown haze, they escaped notice, or they would surely have been forced to leave.

Near the end of the corridor, Raymond twisted open an unmarked door. Behind it lay a second set of stairs, musty and obviously little used.

"You know your way around, don't you?" Chance growled, removing his cummerbund and holding it over his mouth to filter the smoke. "How on earth did you figure all this out?"

"I did my research." Struggling against a fit of coughing, Ray looked older than ever before, with no trace of the customary cockiness. "For what it's worth, I'm sorry. I never meant any harm."

Even before Chance was born, he'd been the object of his father's schemes and manipulations. Over the past dozen years, he'd made sacrifices and taken risks, fighting Ray at every turn to stick to what was right.

Now the man had circumvented him and endangered Harry's life, and Lois's, as well. It seemed a bit late for repentance.

"Don't ask me to forgive you. Not right now." Pushing past his father, Chance strode up the stairs.

On the first floor, the club had still been illuminated, but the staircase was dark except for a few low-placed red emergency lights. Silently Chance cursed himself for forgetting to bring a flashlight. He'd leapt out of the car without a thought except to find Harry.

The smoke grew thicker as they climbed, stinging his throat and eyes. At the second-story landing, Chance halted, feeling heat billowing down from the attic.

They could go no farther.

TARA'S EYES SMARTED and her skin felt as if it were blistering. Scarcely aware of the firemen hooking up hoses and raising a ladder toward the attic, she struggled to remain in Chance's consciousness.

"What is happening?" asked Rajeev. "Does he need help? I will go in. This is my fault."

Exhausted, she released her mental grasp. Cool air washed over her in a burst of relief. "The attic's engulfed. They can't go up there."

"Surely Lois has brought the boy down by now," Vareena said.

"Then where are they?" Tara asked. "Chance should have seen them on the stairs."

"Perhaps they have come out on the other side," Rajeev said. "I will go around and look."

"I will check in the other direction." Vareena started off.

"Thanks," Tara called after them both. "That would help." After watching the pair depart, she let her eyelids drift shut as she tried to gather her thoughts.

"Excuse me, miss." It was one of the firefighters. "You'll need to leave the area."

"My son is inside!" she protested. "And my husband went in searching for him." The word *husband* slipped out, and she didn't bother to correct it.

"We knew about a boy and a woman missing in the attic," he said. "You mean there are others?"

"Two men," she said. "They're on a hidden staircase. They're trying to reach the top floor but there's too much heat."

The firefighter hurried off. Thank goodness he hadn't insisted she leave, or asked how she knew so much.

If only Harry would make mental contact with her or Chance, Tara thought. But although the boy could read minds and even exert influence over people, apparently he hadn't developed the ability to send his own thoughts to others.

This link between her and Chance was something rare. All she could hope was that its ultimate effect wouldn't be tragedy.

If they hadn't been drawn together on that Halloween night, Harry would never have been born. Each of them would have led a different life, but would that have been so terrible?

By now she might have married some other man and had other children. Would they have meant as much to her as Chance and Harry? Would she have missed the deeper connection, or been content with what she had?

Tara didn't know the answers. She didn't know what she would do if she lost her son or Chance, or both. She couldn't think about that now. She had to clear her mind, and hope that somehow she could find a way to help.

WHEN HE LOST his sense of Tara's presence, it worried Chance at first. He wished he knew whether she was simply distracted, or had become unable to contact him.

In either case, he needed to try to sense his son's thoughts. Shouldering his way out of the staircase and into the second-floor corridor, he crouched down where the air was clearer and formed a picture of Harry in his mind. The key was to open his consciousness and allow the contact to establish itself.

It wasn't working. Except for his unique link with Tara, Chance had never before tried to reach someone who wasn't within sight, and the disorienting effects of smoke and heat made it doubly hard to concentrate.

Then he felt Tara rejoin him. Oxygen cleared away the haze in his brain and his mind came to a sharp focus. It was as if he could not only feel her but breathe with her.

An unnamed power was fusing their spirits, boosting Chance's ability to reach out. As he released his tension and opened himself to receive contact, he caught a fleeting hint of fear. Was he tapping into his son's thoughts or mistaking his own emotions for telepathic communication?

Then the fear returned, plus more. Confusion. Determination. Concern for Lois.

Bits and pieces came to him, not clearly enough to provide a picture of the missing pair, but at least he knew they were still alive. The one fact that reached him clearly was that Harry and Lois had found a third staircase, closer to the fire's origin.

Chance strained to stay with the child's mind. The sensations kept slipping away, but he had to learn more. He needed at least a general idea of where the two had gone, or he would never have time to find them.

Help me, Tara.

A tingling across his skin gave him the odd impression of a ghostly figure overlying his body. Then, with a cooling sigh and a subliminal buzz, their spirits merged.

With the boost from their combined strength, he caught an image of Harry and Lois staggering down from the attic until the staircase became too smoke filled for them to reach the ground floor. They emerged here, on the second floor.

Rising, Chance shouted their names, then realized he must have seen something that had happened earlier. Otherwise, he would have heard or spotted the pair by now. But where had they gone?

He struggled to visualize which room they had entered, but exhaustion thinned the connection with Tara. Drained and starting to cough, he couldn't find her again.

"We need to search the rooms, fast." He turned, expecting to find Ray behind him, but the man wasn't there. A glance at the landing showed that he wasn't waiting on the stairs, either.

How like the man to have fled, just when he was needed most! Restraining his anger, Chance returned his attention to the corridor.

He didn't have more than a few minutes to search before he himself would be overcome. He would have to check the rooms and hope the pair were in plain sight.

The first room proved to be an office, crammed with desks and filing cabinets. Chance shouted their names hoarsely, but there was no answer.

Pulling the cummerbund tighter around his mouth, he moved on.

A GREAT MANTLE of weariness pressed down on Tara. She, too, had seen Harry and Lois stagger from the stairs into the second-floor hallway, but where were they?

She tried to reach out, to give Chance her strength, but received only an impression of choking darkness. It had an odd familiarity, not from the distant past but from something she'd seen recently.

A videotape on fire preparedness. She'd checked it out of the library a few months ago to watch with her son. It had been one of those endless motherly precautions, like posting CPR instructions on the refrigerator.

The video's horrifying depiction of roiling darkness had given her nightmares. Harry hadn't been fazed, though.

A comment he'd made tickled the back of her mind, as hard to grasp as a fading dream. What was it? What had he said?

"Why don't the people get in the bathtub?"

That was it! He'd been convinced that hiding in a tub of water was the best protection from a fire. Although Tara had pointed out the deadliness of smoke inhalation, Harry hadn't understood.

Was it possible the notion had stuck in his mind? She had to let Chance know.

IT WAS TAKING LONGER than he expected to go through the rooms. Once Chance thought he saw a shadow move, and shoved aside several boxes before he realized it had been caused by lights outside the window.

There were half a dozen more rooms, and he was running out of air. He still hadn't seen any firemen on this floor. Why didn't they come racing up the main staircase, which must connect with the other end of the hallway?

As he thrust his way into yet another office, the chilling truth struck him. The main staircase didn't reach this corridor. There must be another section of second floor, separated by the two- and three-story meeting and ball-rooms. Unless the firemen stumbled across one of the two smaller staircases, they wouldn't even know this area existed until too late.

Even keeping close to the floor barely provided enough air. Sputtering and gasping, Chance knew he could investigate one more chamber at most.

Bathtub.

He heard the word, and knew the communication came from Tara. It was all she could get through to him.

Somehow, she had figured out where Harry was. Now if Chance could only find him.

Bypassing the next two offices, he staggered toward a narrow door. It was too dark to read, but his fingers traced the letters *R* and *E*.

Rest room.

He staggered inside, peering through the haze. There were two toilet stalls and a sink but no tub. Bitterness churned as he realized that, even if Harry had come here, the boy wouldn't have found what he was seeking.

But this was an old house. Maybe the tub lay in an adjacent room, out of sight.

Stumbling around the stalls, he saw that he'd guessed right. Behind them stood a small door that he would otherwise have mistaken for a closet.

"Harry? Lois?" Wrenching it open, Chance stepped onto a tiled surface.

Floodlights from outside shone through a narrow window onto an old-fashioned claw-footed tub filled with water. In the distorted shadows, he thought for a moment it was empty, then realized he was seeing an almost solid mass formed by two bodies intertwined.

"Daddy!" A little voice raised goose bumps across his flesh.

"Chance!" Lois tried to rise, slipped and grabbed the edge of the tub.

He pulled them both from the water. The splash of wetness against his clothing felt wonderful, but it couldn't compare with the exultation of seeing their eager faces.

Harry nestled into his father's arms. "You saved us!"

"Thank heavens you're here." Trembling and soaked, Lois didn't look much older than the boy. "I can't believe we're safe!"

The danger was far from past, however. They still had to get out of here.

Chance doubted they'd be able to go back the way he'd come. Without giving it any more thought, he yanked at the double-hung sash window.

It stuck. Two more shoulder-straining jerks and he shoved it open. Leaning out, he waved and shouted, but with all the commotion, he couldn't make himself heard.

He didn't need to. Whether she'd seen him or sensed him, Tara noticed him at once. With a signal of recognition, she ran toward one of the firefighters.

It seemed to take forever, but must have been no more than a few minutes, before a ladder reached them. With a fireman's assistance, Chance boosted Harry out the window, followed by a shivering Lois.

He himself was coughing so hard, he nearly fell on the way down, but he wasn't going to give up now. Only when his feet made contact with the pavement did he allow himself to stagger in exhaustion.

A fire captain caught him. "Is everyone out, sir?" the man asked.

About to answer in the affirmative, Chance hesitated.

"My father went up with me and then he vanished. I assumed he came downstairs."

"What does your father look like, sir?" the captain queried, when a shout came from the attic. Above, a fire-fighter emerged onto a ladder with a large body draped over his shoulder.

Instead of fleeing, Raymond must have thrust his way into the thick of danger. He'd been trying to find his niece and grandson in the attic.

He was hurt but alive, one of the firefighters said a few minutes later. That was the last thing Chance heard before he blacked out.

Chapter Sixteen

"It is a time for new beginnings." Great-aunt Cynda plopped her crystal ball onto the table beside Raymond's hospital bed.

"I suppose it is." Tara stifled a yawn. She'd spent the night at Harry's bedside while he, Chance and Lois were under observation and Ray was treated for smoke inhalation and second-degree burns.

The boy was napping this morning, and Tara had decided to accompany Cynda as she visited the others. They'd left Chance when his doctor arrived, and picked up Lois en route to the burn unit.

"Things will be different now," Cynda announced. "Very different indeed."

"You've seen the future?" Lois asked. Her hands, which had been blistered last night, were thrust deep into the pockets of her bathrobe.

"I don't need to see the future. It's clear to anyone." The older woman stepped away from the crystal ball. "I thought my nephew might want to practice with this while he's laid up. He needs to find a better outlet for his energies than trying to manipulate other people."

From his mummylike swathe of bandages, Raymond eyed her ruefully. He was doped up with painkillers, but the doctor had said the burns weren't severe enough to be life threatening and he should make a full recovery.

"I guess we all need a better outlet for our energies," Lois admitted. "Tara, I'm sorry. I've been so stupid and selfish."

"At least it came out okay," Tara said. "I'm glad you weren't hurt more seriously."

"Thanks to Harry." The young woman grimaced. "He's the one who kept calm, not me. He's a very special little boy, and not because of any darn mind-reading abilities. Phooey on that."

"I'm glad to see you've had a change of heart," Cynda told her granddaughter. "And a change of career, too, I hope."

Ray mumbled beneath his bandages.

"You stay out of this," said Cynda.

"Oh, let the mummy speak." Lois shot her boss a skeptical glance. "Well?"

The words were slurred and only partly audible. "Somebody has to mumble mumble and take over the business. Lois has the right mumble."

"You're retiring? Good!" Cynda gave his bandaged leg a thump. "New beginnings, just as I said!"

"I've got a lot to learn about the company." Lois sighed. "You have executives who are a lot more qualified than I am. But maybe I'll stick around and work my way up."

"You can do it," said Cynda. "*Without* any sneaky stuff."

"Absolutely," Lois agreed. "By the way, Raymond, what did Victor Moustaki have to say about last night's fiasco?"

"Surely he isn't taking phone calls!" Cynda protested.

"I have it on good authority he took this one," said

her granddaughter. "I talked to his secretary this morning."

"He mumble mumble that we were spying mumble mumble cussed me out. The deal's off."

"Serves you right." Cynda's peppery response, far from angering Raymond, raised a low chuckle.

"I'm a changed man. I'll never mumble mumble again."

"We'll see about that." She gave him a stern look.

After a few minutes, Tara excused herself and made her way to Harry's room. She found her son awake, playing with a menagerie of stuffed animals sent by a kind-hearted public. The dramatic rescue had appeared on the late news and in this morning's papers.

The coverage had reached as far as Kentucky. Tara's father had called earlier, full of concern. He'd invited her, Harry and Chance to come visit his new family, and she'd said they would, when things settled down.

Her father's rejection when she'd needed him most could never entirely be erased, but neither could the ties between them. Tara was glad her son would have a chance to know both his grandfathers.

"How's Daddy?" the boy asked as she sat down.

"He's fine. You should both be coming home today," Tara said. "You're a hero. Did you know that?"

He grinned. "I can't wait to tell Al and Sammi!"

"I'll bet they already know." She stroked a shock of brown hair from his forehead. Aside from some bruises, he'd come through the ordeal remarkably unscathed. "You saved Lois's life."

His expression grew serious. "It was Dad who saved us. And you did, too, figuring out about the bathtub. Mom?"

"Yes, sweetie?"

"I thought I was real powerful, because of the stuff I can do. But it wasn't much use against a fire, was it?"

She scooped her son into her arms. "Magical powers are no substitute for good judgment and courage. And you showed both of those last night."

A nurse came in with discharge papers, and there was no more time for quiet talk. Tara found herself bustling through the hospital, making sure all the paperwork was completed for Chance as well as for Harry. She barely had time to say goodbye to Cynda and Lois.

Raymond was undergoing therapy, but she would visit him tomorrow. Having seen how he'd risked his life to try to save Harry and Lois, Tara was willing to give him a second chance. She doubted he would turn into a model grandfather, but she suspected last night's lesson would stick.

Rajeev arrived with the Lexus to collect the three of them. On the way home, Harry filled their ears with chatter about his new stuffed animals. Each was named after a video-game character: there were monkeys named Diddy and Dixie and bears named Mario and Luigi.

Chance, sitting in front beside Rajeev, nodded and gave his son an occasional half smile over his shoulder. His face betraying his exhaustion, he hadn't said much this morning. The doctor had cautioned that last night's brush with death must have been traumatic, and that he would show some lingering effects.

When Harry finished, Rajeev took over, explaining that the remainder of the competition had been scheduled for the following week. "Now that we have more experience, I am sure we will win," he said. "We have got our feet wet. Or sooty. Or something."

They arrived home to find the house filled with the

aroma of baking. Proudly, Vareena presented them with an array of spicy vegetable-filled pastries for lunch.

Afterward, following doctor's orders, Chance and Harry both went to bed. Tara checked the answering machine and returned phone calls from Chance's staff and a number of friends, including Denise. She assured them that everyone was fine.

She wished she felt more confident about that herself. Something had changed last night between her and Chance. Aunt Cynda had been right; there'd been unfinished business between them from a past life.

From the moment they'd met, fate had pushed and dragged Tara and Chance toward last night's terrifying turn of events. They had survived the fire and, at least in a symbolic sense, overcome the tyrant. The circle had been completed.

But what did that leave? At the hospital, Tara hadn't felt the sensual pull that would shift her into Chance's awareness. That connection had vanished, as if silence had fallen between them.

These past months, she'd been afraid of making love with him, afraid of what might happen when they merged. She ought to feel relieved. With the old bonds removed, she was free.

But seeing Chance in deadly peril had made her realize that life would never be complete without him. The tender, teasing way he looked at her, the touch of his hands, the herbal scent of him had become a part of her.

New beginnings. She hoped Cynda was right this time, as well. But where did they start? And how could she be sure that Chance would want to begin again?

It didn't make Tara feel any better when he took dinner in his room. She and Harry ate in the kitchen with Rajeev and Vareena.

Although she enjoyed their company, it was a relief to learn that the pair would be leaving after dinner to drive to San Diego. A cousin from India had called to say he was flying into town unexpectedly on business, and hoped they could meet him. His only free time would be early the next morning.

"We haven't seen him in three years," Vareena explained.

"That's a long way to come for such a short visit," Tara said as she helped collect the dishes.

"He is going also to Chicago and New York." Rajeev tucked leftovers into plastic containers. "Then he will return home by way of Europe."

"We want to show him our dancing," Vareena said. "We will take the boom box."

"And now we must pack," said her brother. "We return tomorrow afternoon."

"There's no hurry. I can handle things here." Much as she liked the pair, Tara wanted some time alone with Chance. They needed to talk and perhaps make some painful decisions.

With the psychic link severed, it would be awkward for her to stay here. Of course, Chance would always be Harry's father, and they would never forget what they'd shared, but she was beginning to wonder if their "new beginnings" weren't destined to be separate.

Escorting Harry back to their quarters, Tara felt a spurt of determination. She didn't want to be some figure from Chance's past. She didn't just want to be his coparent, either. She wanted the whole man.

These past months, their mental link had, in a way, interfered with establishing a normal relationship. But that didn't mean it couldn't be done.

Because of his magic powers, Chance might be more

sensitive than she was to the changes that had occurred last night, and he'd certainly suffered more physical trauma. So it was up to Tara to take the first step.

She read Harry a story and waited until he fell asleep. Then she went into her bedroom to brush her hair and freshen her makeup.

The rainbow-hued suit from last night's dinner waited on a hanger for a trip to the dry cleaners. Gazing at it, she realized that she no longer felt it had been designed for someone more sophisticated and elegant. In the course of the past twenty-four hours, Tara had become that woman.

Her elbows and knees had stopped feeling as if they had minds of their own. Her body seemed not too thin but just right. Even her hair fell smoothly into place.

What about Chance? she wondered. Had his perceptions of himself altered, too?

More curious than apprehensive, she changed from jeans and a blouse into a simple black jersey sheath. Then she strolled toward his suite, taking a shortcut through the courtyard.

In the early-summer twilight, she felt the nearness of living things. Trees and flowers scented the air, and an errant bee hummed past, late to the hive. A cricket chirped hopefully from an unseen location.

She almost didn't see Chance standing near the staircase, his muscular body a silhouette among shadows. He watched her with a guarded expression.

"Do you feel different?" she asked.

Warmth gleamed in his silver eyes. "A little. Mostly I was worried about how you would feel."

"Harry's asleep," she said. "Rajeev and Vareena went to San Diego to see a relative."

"It would seem that the night is ours." He rested one arm on the ironwork railing.

This was the first time she had ever been able to perceive Chance objectively. He was strikingly handsome, she realized, even without unseen forces making her desire him. Although not unusually tall, his classical build and knowing air made him dominate the space around him.

"It's amazing how relaxing this is," he murmured.

"What do you mean?"

"I've had to maintain a barrier between us. It's something I can do with part of my mind, and often I was hardly aware of it. But it was always there."

How ironic, she thought. Losing their psychic connection had meant gaining a different kind of openness.

"This was where we first met." He stepped forward, extending his hand. "Hello, I'm Chance Powers."

"I'm Tara Blayne." As she shook it, the air between them zinged with chemical reactions.

"Welcome to my Halloween party," he said.

"Oh, dear." She smiled. "I think my girlfriend and I have come to the wrong place."

"Then let's make sure it turns out to be the right one," he said.

MAGIC HAD BEEN many things to Chance, and brought him many experiences. But he had never known anything like this.

When he put his arms around Tara, she melted into him without reservation. Their mouths met with a spark, and her arms twined around his neck in sultry invitation. This was a different kind of magic from what he had known before. Deeper and purer.

They drifted up the stairs, pausing for a kiss, an

embrace, a whisper of tender longings. Her hair brushed his cheek, soft as an angel's wing.

The desire that she aroused was more urgent than he had felt before, yet he wanted to prolong this sensuous anticipation as long as possible. This time, when they made love, they would enter a new world together.

Last time, they had understood nothing. This time, he thought with a flash of humility, they understood only a little more. It would take the rest of their lives to explore the realm that can be created between one man and one woman.

The tower admitted them at a touch. He murmured some words, and a bed appeared.

At the same time, Chance got the impression that this was no longer a room but a glade in a forest. Beneath tall straight trees glowed colors as bright as stained glass—the emerald green of the forest floor, the flashing scarlet of enchanted birds.

He and Tara sank onto a bed as soft as goose down. In some ways she was a stranger to him; in others, his dearest friend and partner.

With the perceptions of a man instead of a magician, he relished the flush on her cheeks and the velvet of her skin as he smoothed away the clingy dress. With a twist and a shrug, he removed his own shirt and pants.

Tara ran her hand up his hip and along his ribs. "I feel as if this were our first time."

"It is," he said.

She slipped out of her undergarments, showing no trace of self-consciousness as he drank in the long lines of her body. Her small firm breasts invited his hands to cup them, and, when he did, she sucked in a shuddering breath.

Gently Chance pulled her to him. She curved onto his

lap, her mouth meeting his and her bare body arched against his naked chest.

He could read her pleasure in the subtle shift of expressions on her face. There was no need to enter her awareness through any supernatural means.

Chance experienced his own reactions more keenly than ever before: the pulsing heat in his blood, the half-painful, half-joyous intensity of his arousal. This time, he had something to give Tara, and she to give him, precisely because they remained separate.

Laying her across the bed, he explored her body with his hands and mouth. She responded with fierce eagerness, tantalizing him until Chance could bear the delay no longer.

When he thrust within her, it thrilled him to gauge his ability to please by the soft gasps that arose from her. And when she responded with a rhythmic shifting matched to the tempo of his breathing, he soared into ecstasy.

They became the soul of the forest, vibrant and throbbing as they lost themselves in each other. Chance flew beyond himself, soaring over the green canopy into an explosion of white light.

Tara's soft cries eased into moans of satisfaction. Lying beside her, Chance let fulfillment wash over him.

She pillowed her head against his shoulder. The air of the tower came alive with their residual heat and the lingering impression of trees in a foreign land, long ago and far away.

"I wonder…" he murmured.

"Hmm?"

"Last time, we conceived Harry," he said.

"I wouldn't mind having a daughter," she said. He

could feel her smile against his bare skin. "Or another little boy."

"If not, we'll just have to go on trying." He kept his tone deadpan.

"What a sacrifice," said Tara.

Chance pulled up the covers, protecting her from the cool air. "The computer can produce a desk or a book-shelf or a bureau, but there's one very important thing I forgot to build into this room."

"What's that?" she asked sleepily.

"A wedding ring." He muffled a yawn. "I guess we'll have to buy one the old-fashioned way, at a jewelry store. What do you think?"

"I'm not moving," Tara said.

"I didn't mean tonight!"

"Well, thank goodness."

As he tightened his grip around the woman he loved, Chance thought of one more thing. "Computer," he said. "Is Harry all right?"

"Subject child remains in bed," said the nasal tenor. "There are no signs of distress."

"Just make sure everything's locked up, then," said Chance.

"I have already done so, o lordly one."

"Good night, then." In the quiet that followed, sleep began to blur the edges of his consciousness.

"Excuse me," said the house.

"Yes?" He hoped the computer wasn't going to enu-merate the leftovers in the refrigerator. He hadn't yet fig-ured out a way to teach the thing timing.

"I thought the Tara person would want to know," it said.

Tara yawned beside him. "Know what?"

"I've picked a name."

"You have?" She propped herself on her elbows. "What is it?"

"It's Home," said the house. "Do you like it?"

"It's perfect," Tara said. "Good night, Home."

"Good night, Tara person. And noble master."

Across the courtyard, a light went out in the kitchen. A mechanical hum signaled that the computer was double-checking the alarm system.

Then even Home grew quiet, and the magic of the night cast its spell over this enchanted place.

EVER HAD ONE OF THOSE DAYS?

TO DO:

- ☑ late for a super-important meeting, you discover the cat has eaten your panty hose

- ☑ while you work through lunch, the rest of the gang goes out and finds a one-hour, once-in-a-lifetime 90% off sale at the most exclusive store in town (Oh, and they also get to meet Brad Pitt who's filming a movie across the street.)

- ☑ you discover that your intimate phone call with your boyfriend was on company-wide intercom

- ☑ finally at the end of a long and exasperating day, you escape from it all with an entertaining, humorous and always romantic Love & Laughter book!

ENJOY
LOVE & LAUGHTER™
EVERY DAY!

For a preview, turn the page....

Here's a sneak peek at
Colleen Collins's RIGHT CHEST, WRONG NAME
Available August 1997...

"DARLING, YOU SOUND like a broken cappuccino machine," murmured Charlotte, her voice oozing disapproval.

Russell juggled the receiver while attempting to sit up in bed, but couldn't. If he *sounded* like a wreck over the phone, he could only imagine what he looked like.

"What mischief did you and your friends get into at your bachelor's party last night?" she continued.

She always had a way of saying "your friends" as though they were a pack of degenerate water buffalo. Professors deserved to be several notches higher up on the food chain, he thought. Which he would have said if his tongue wasn't swollen to twice its size.

"You didn't do anything...bad...did you, Russell?"

"Bad." His laugh came out like a bark.

"Bad as in *naughty*."

He heard her piqued tone but knew she'd never admit to such a base emotion as jealousy. Charlotte Maday, the woman he was to wed in a week, came from a family who bled blue. Exhibiting raw emotion was akin to burping in public.

After agreeing to be at her parents' pool party by noon,

he untangled himself from the bed sheets and stumbled to the bathroom.

"Pool party," he reminded himself. He'd put on his best front and accommodate Char's request. Make the family rounds, exchange a few pleasantries, play the role she liked best: the erudite, cultured English literature professor. After fulfilling his duties, he'd slink into some lawn chair, preferably one in the shade, and nurse his hangover.

He tossed back a few aspirin and splashed cold water on his face. Grappling for a towel, he squinted into the mirror.

Then he jerked upright and stared at his reflection, blinking back drops of water. "Good Lord. They stuck me in a wind tunnel."

His hair, usually neatly parted and combed, sprang from his head as though he'd been struck by lightning. "Can too many Wild Turkeys do that?" he asked himself as he stared with horror at his reflection.

Something caught his eye in the mirror. Russell's gaze dropped.

"What in the—"

Over his pectoral muscle was a small patch of white. A bandage. Gingerly, he pulled it off.

Underneath, on his skin, was not a wound but a small, neat drawing.

"A red heart?" His voice cracked on the word *heart*. Something—a word?—was scrawled across it.

"Good Lord," he croaked. "I got a tattoo. A heart tattoo with the name Liz on it."

Not Charlotte. Liz!

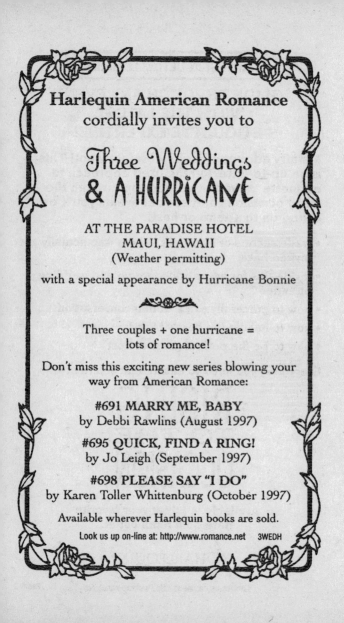

Harlequin American Romance
cordially invites you to

Three Weddings
& A HURRICANE

AT THE PARADISE HOTEL
MAUI, HAWAII
(Weather permitting)

with a special appearance by Hurricane Bonnie

Three couples + one hurricane =
lots of romance!

Don't miss this exciting new series blowing your
way from American Romance:

#691 MARRY ME, BABY
by Debbi Rawlins (August 1997)

#695 QUICK, FIND A RING!
by Jo Leigh (September 1997)

#698 PLEASE SAY "I DO"
by Karen Toller Whittenburg (October 1997)

Available wherever Harlequin books are sold.

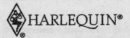

HARLEQUIN WOMEN KNOW ROMANCE WHEN THEY SEE IT.

Let's Celebrate!

LOVE & LAUGHTER™

invites you to the party of the season!

Grab your popcorn and be prepared to laugh as we celebrate with **LOVE & LAUGHTER**.

Harlequin's newest series is going Hollywood!

Let us make you laugh with three months of terrific books, authors and romance, plus a chance to win a FREE 15-copy video collection of the best romantic comedies ever made.

For more details look in the back pages of any Love & Laughter title, from July to September, at your favorite retail outlet.

Don't forget the popcorn!

Available wherever
Harlequin books are sold.

 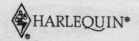 HARLEQUIN®

Look us up on-line at: http://www.romance.net

LLCELEB